SECRET DADDY NEXT DOOR

AN ENEMIES TO LOVERS ROMANCE

CALLIE STEVENS

ONE

DARA

Steady, Dara...steady...

I position the small figurine depicting a little family of four bundled up in winter gear on the top tier of the cake, carefully jiggling it until it's perfectly level.

"There we go." I draw back and admire my precision with pride. This is the first wedding cake I've made all on my own from the first consultation all the way down to the finishing touches. I owe Rye big time for getting me this gig.

I tilt my head to the side and narrow my eyes. Something is missing.

"Flowers! The flowers!" I scramble around to the box of pansies Rye sourced herself. The purple and yellow-faced flowers will look perfect scattered around the cake. I position them hurriedly. I wanted to have this done before the reception started so that I could focus on arranging the platters of smaller desserts that will be brought out after dinner service.

"Can we come in?"

I look up and grin. Rye is peeking into the pastry kitchen with Ivy on her hip. The two of them are like twins with their dark hair. Ivy's getting so big too, almost one year old. Time seriously flies.

"Of course! My two favorite girls are always welcome in my kitchen!"

Rye blushes. "Well, I brought some company."

The door opens wider, revealing the whole Hawthorn family, newlywed couple included.

"Oh, yikes!" I step in front of the cake. "It's not finished. I'm still putting the flowers on."

"I just wanted to show off your work before the reception starts."

I swallow and take a deep breath. "Okay. Just remember it's not –"

"Totally done," Ash says with a smile. "We got it, Dara."

I smile bashfully and step aside, letting them cast their eyes on the cake as they file into the pastry kitchen. The kitchen felt so big before the Hawthorns entered. Now, it feels like a cramped forest.

Rye scans her family and gestures to each of them. "Dara, you know Ash, obviously. And this is his son, Oliver–"

Oliver, taller than tall with dark features and pouty lips, holds his hand out to me. "Nice to meet you, Dara."

I shake his hand. "You too."

"And this is June and Jarred."

The happy couple look beautiful together and already have their hands full with June holding their three-month-old baby boy and Jarred balancing his little girl, Piper, on his hip. They make a beautiful couple. June wears a simple satin gown that shows off her collarbone, and Jarred's wearing a navy suit that bring out his eyes.

"And this is–" Rye stops. "Where's Keifer?"

Ash scans everyone as if he's doing a headcount. "He was just with us."

"He had to take a phone call," Oliver clarifies, and then says to me, "He's going on a work trip tomorrow and is getting everything in line."

I smile. "I'm not offended."

"We're sorry we couldn't meet with you personally," June apologizes, her big eyes hypnotic with their different colors. She bounces her baby up and down. He has the same eyes as her. "As you can see, we had our hands full."

"But clearly, Rye gave you all the help you need. I mean, look at the topper," Jarred says, pointing to the figurine on the top of the cake.

Little Piper squeals. "That's us! That's Daddy and Mommy and Hayden and that's me!"

"How did you do that?" June asks with wide eyes.

I smile. "Well, it's just a lot of sugar and food coloring."

Rye rolls her eyes. "She's being modest. Dara is the best baker I know. There's a reason we're going into business together."

Rye convinced me to move down to Chicago shortly after she opened her flower shop. There was a property next door that opened up with a kitchen. She suggested I could come down and open my own place next door to her shop. That way, we could offer a package deal for event planning too. I thought it was a great idea. The only issue has been money. Rye has eagerly offered to pay for everything (after all, she's now a billionaire), but I can't accept that. The store is mine, and I want it to feel that way too. Luckily, I have a job lined up with one of the foremost pastry shops in the city that will allow me to build up my capital.

And this gig is definitely paying well. It was a rush order, after all.

"Why are there flowers on the cake?" Piper asks.

Ivy starts to reach for one. Rye tries to hold her back but I hand a pansy to Ivy and Piper. "You can eat them! That's why."

Piper immediately sticks it in her mouth while Ivy is more discerning. She chews and then makes a face. "Yuck."

"Not the most adventurous eater, as you can tell," Jarred says.

"Maybe someday," I smile.

"So, listen, after you're done back here, you have to come out and join the party, okay?" Rye asks.

I shake my head. "I don't want to impose."

"Don't be silly! You're practically a part of the family, Dara," Ash says.

My heart grows. I'd love to be a part of their family. Just hearing about how supportive they all are to one another and their famous Sunday night dinners makes me want a little piece of the action. It's been a long time since I've gotten to sit around a dinner table with people I called family. "Well, alright. I'll come out when I'm done back here. Might be a while, though. I still have to work on the cream puffs."

"Whenever you're done, come on out and have a drink. Relax. You've clearly been working extremely hard." Ash pats my shoulder and then jerks his head back toward the kitchen door. "You two better get out there for your entrance."

Jarred and June nod, thank me profusely once more, and then head out of the kitchen with their little family, trying to decide if their baby boy, Hayden, needs to be changed before the reception. Oliver gives me one more nod and then follows.

Ivy squirms, reaching her arms out to her father. Ash

takes her eagerly. "I'll give you two a moment alone."

"Thanks, honey."

Ash kisses Rye on the crown of her head before heading out of the room.

Finally, alone, the two of us grab hands and squeal excitedly.

"Thank you, thank you, thank you!" Rye cries out and hugs me tightly.

"Thank *you*!"

"No! You have no idea how helpful this is. When Jarred and June said they wanted to get married in January, I had no idea how we'd get it all done. But here you are." Rye touches my cheek. "You're the best, Dar."

I shake my head. "Are you kidding? You're the one who gave me a reason to come out to Chicago. I have you to thank."

"We're going to have so much fun together."

"Yes. And if you ever need a babysitter –"

"Obviously, I'll call you. Ivy needs her Auntie Dara time."

We hug again.

"Seriously, when you're done, come out and party. I'm not going to have you relegated to the kitchen the whole night, especially when you look like that!"

I look down at my outfit. Under my apron, I'm wearing an emerald V-neck dress that goes a little past my knees. It's classy, but a little bit sexy too.

"Trust me, you're going to catch some eyes out there. So, don't stay hidden for too long." Rye winks at me and then rushes out of the kitchen when she hears the DJ starting to announce the wedding party.

I smile to myself. Chicago is going to be an amazing adventure. I can feel it.

TWO

KEIFER

"We'll have a driver waiting for you when you arrive, Mr. Hawthorn."

I pace back and forth down a cobblestone pathway. I can't believe I had to step away from my brother and best friend's wedding to take such a useless phone call. Why aren't they emailing this information instead of having both of us waste time like this? And yet, here I am.

"Great. Will there be a car waiting for me?"

"Yes. Of course."

"Something nice, right?"

Cass Jameson, CEO of Jameson Technologies, chuckles on the other end of the phone. "Yes, Mr. Hawthorn. Something nice. If you have a request, I'm happy to relay that to my assistant."

"No, no. I'll trust you. I like being surprised." *Sometimes.*

I slip my suit jacket off; the heat of the conservatory is getting to me. I'm surrounded by towering tropical plants and trees, brightly colored flowers. It's a perfect location for a wedding, not a place to take a work phone call when you're supposed to be having fun at said wedding. "What else can I do for you, Mr. Jameson?"

For two months, I'm headed down to San Diego to shadow at Jameson Technologies on behalf of my dad's company, Hawthorn Incorporated. As the chief operating officer, I'm constantly looking for improvements to streamline our processes. Given how crazy everything has been the past two years, we're in need of a total revamp and overhaul. Jameson Technologies is top ranked in that regard and, luckily for us, Dad and Cass are old friends. I'm going down to take notes and see what I can bring back to Hawthorn to make things better for us.

That's the boring part. The fun part is it's basically like a two-month vacation in sunny California. I get to escape the Chicago winter and all the depressing weather and mood swings that come with it. Should be fun.

"I want to go through the order of operations for Monday. It's a busy day and I don't want you to get lost in the fray."

I try not to sigh. I need to get back to the wedding. I peer through the windows of the conservatory to the ballroom on the other side of the glass door. I missed the entrances and dinner service is getting started. My family is all stationed at a table together. The Hawthorn clan seems to be growing by the day. And if I'm honest, it's going to be nice to get a break from them too.

Don't get me wrong, I love them all. And I'm definitely going to miss the kids. But everyone's been so wrapped up in their own bullshit that I feel like I'm just getting in the way. Even Oliver, who is unattached just like me, is always running after his best friend, Trevor, trying to pick up the pieces of his failed relationship with Rowan.

It'll be good to get some time away from them. Absence makes the heart grow fonder, after all.

"Give it to me, Cass."

When I finally get back to the reception, they're already halfway through dinner service. Luckily, no one seems upset with me. It's not until Hayden, my new nephew, sees me and reaches in my direction that June even notices I've arrived at the table.

"There you are!" she says with a smile.

"Surprise. I'm still here."

June releases Hayden into my arms.

"Hey little man. How you doin'? You miss Uncle Keif?"

Hayden kicks his chubby legs and gurgles, spit bubbling up in his little red mouth.

"Is everything okay?" June asks.

"Yeah, yeah. Just work stuff. I'm sorry. I'm not meaning to be distracted but–"

"Keifer, it's okay." She reaches out and squeezes my arm. "You know I don't mind."

I know she doesn't, but I do. I've tried to be there for her every step of this process. From finding out she was pregnant, to her and Jarred finally getting their shit together and admitting their feelings, to being on babysitting duty the day Hayden was born. Now, it's their wedding day, and I feel like my head is in too many places.

"How are you feeling?" I ask her, bouncing my godson in my arms.

She grins and shrugs. Oooh, she's definitely had a lot of champagne already. "I need to eat something."

"You definitely do. There's still a whole lot of reception left."

June rests her rosy face in her hand. Jarred leans over and kisses the side of her head. "Doesn't she look beautiful, Keifer?"

"Unlike you, Jarred, June is like a sister to me, and calling her beautiful would definitely make things weird."

June hits my arm with the back of her hand. I've already told her how beautiful she looks earlier, before the ceremony. It does feel weird to compliment her looks when to me, she's like the twin sister I never had. But it's true, she's totally glowing. And the two of them together make such a handsome couple.

I can't help but wonder when it will be my turn.

"So, what do you think, Keif? You going to make it back from California?" Jarred asks, taking a swig of his whisky on the rocks.

"What do you mean?"

"You're not going to get too starry eyed over those California girls? Not going to make us find a new COO, are you?"

"Yeah, right." I scoff. "No, Chicago's home. I'm not going anywhere. But..."

"But a little fun never killed a man." Jeez, Jarred's already tipsy too. They've got kids. They're going to be hurting tomorrow morning, that's for sure.

"Maybe a little fun, but not too much. I'm not looking for anything. You know that." Hayden reaches up toward my face and I kiss his little hand. "Even though you're so cute, I'm not looking to losing my beauty sleep quite yet, little man."

June leans on Jarred's shoulder, wrapping her hand

around his arm. "You're so good with him, Keif. You're totally ready to be a dad."

"Do not curse me like that, please. Too many things to do, too many places to see. I've got time. I'm only twenty-seven after all."

"I'm just saying, if and when it happens, you'll make a great dad."

Hayden starts to fuss and lets out a loud cry. "You want to take that comment back?" I say, handing him back over to his mother.

Jarred and June laugh, totally blissed out with alcohol and love for their new little family.

Yeah. I want that. So bad. Just not yet. But someday. I've got it all planned out.

I'm able to unwind and enjoy dinner and dessert without worrying about work. Jarred and June's wedding is huge, full of friends and family. I've got my eyes scanning tables left and right, trying to find someone, anyone, who might be a willing distraction for the night.

I'm not usually that kind of guy. Sure, I've had a night here and there with a girl, a couple short-lived relationships, but I'm not usually *looking* to hit it and quit it.

Weddings, though, just bring the energy out of me. Not only is the happy couple rubbing their love in everyone's faces, but *every* couple gets gooey and mushy with each other. It's gross... and I can't help but want some.

I go to the bar for another glass of whisky on the rocks, observing the party with the focus of a big cat on the savanna.

That's when I see her. A woman I haven't seen all night,

with bobbed blonde hair, wearing a dark green dress that plunges right between her breasts. She's sipping champagne all alone on the periphery of the party, nuzzled up against the base of a tropical tree with wide, umbrella-like leaves.

"Your drink, sir?"

I've been so distracted I didn't even realize the bartender had my drink ready. "Th-thank you." I take the drink and throw a couple bills into the tip jar.

When I turn back to look at the woman, I'm almost knocked off my feet. She's looking at me now. Her beautiful hazel eyes look like polished gemstones. And her mouth swiped only with a little bit of gloss is curled into a sweet, inviting smile.

Bingo.

THREE

DARA

When he looks at me, the world stops. I try to smile, hoping I don't look as awkward as I feel.

I've been standing on the outskirts of the party since I finished up with my duties, not really knowing how to make my entrance. Rye is preoccupied with Ash and Ivy and even though I've met the rest of her family, I'd feel uncomfortable making any of them babysit me.

Now, though, I'm thankful for being a wallflower since catching the eye of this tall drink of water. Green eyes, waves of dark blond hair, built tall and lean. I'm light-headed just looking at him.

He smiles back. I resist downing my champagne as fast as possible, but I could use some of that liquid courage ASAP. Although, I've already drank two glasses to pass the time.

I let him come to me. That's something that always works when I'm out at a bar with friends. Don't look too eager or too hungry. Let them know you'll do fine with them or without them.

But something about this guy lets me know I'll do much better *with* him tonight.

"Let me guess. Eve."

I frown.

He gestures to the tree and the thicket of greenery around us. "And this is your garden of Eden."

Once I catch on, I laugh. "Guilty as charged. You're Adam, then?"

"I hope so," he says with a smooth smile.

Okay, we're off to a great start.

"Bride or groom?" he asks with a look over to the crowded dance floor.

I hesitate. "Uh. Both. Or. Neither."

"Are you a party crasher, Eve?" My Adam smirks. I suppose we're really leaning into these nicknames. I don't mind, though. Eve, the very first woman, who tempted Adam into sinning with her. I've never seen myself as much of a seductress, but Adam's already cast me in the role.

I have to play the part.

I laugh. "No, no. Not at all. I'm the... desserts. I did the desserts."

"Oh, no way!"

"Yeah, way." *Dara, stop being weird.* "I just finished up, so I'm having a glass of champagne and..."

"Being bothered by a guy..."

I shake my head. "No, not a bother at all."

He raises his eyebrows, pleasantly surprised. "Oh. Good."

We're both quiet, searching for the next right thing to say. "How about you? Bride or groom."

"Uh. Both."

I narrow my eyes. "Now I have to wonder if *you're* the party crasher."

He chuckles. "No, I just don't like to pick sides."

It's too late to ask for his real name. I think he would've offered it at this point if he wanted it to be known. I don't mind really. It's all part of the fun. I like to collect experiences like stamps. Each one is a sweet reminder of a life well lived. And if there's one thing I'm committed to, it's living my life to the fullest.

"Are you just in town for the wedding or..."

"No, no. I live here. Born and raised," he says with a sigh. "How about you? You must have a business here unless–"

"I'm new to town. My friend got me the gig, so..." I shrug. "I've been living in Wisconsin, which is where I'm from, and I'm going to start a bakery down here in the city."

"Good for you. That's awesome."

"Thank you."

Adam looks down briefly, a lock of hair falling over his forehead. "Your, uh, boyfriend must feel really lucky. I bet you bake for him all the time."

I take a sip of champagne. "No boyfriend." How that wasn't clear already, I'm not sure.

"A beautiful girl like you and no boyfriend? That's a crime."

I blush. "Their loss might be your gain, though." Damn, this champagne really did go to my head. I'm never this forward. Like, *ever*!

"I think you might be right about that." He scans the conservatory once more. "And I believe there's something about the Garden of Eden being full of temptation or something..."

"If this narrative is going to work, we'll need a snake and an apple."

Adam swallows and laughs nervously. "I am resisting hard to make a double entendre."

Snake, like his... seriously, Dara, you're embarrassing yourself.

My eyes dart down to his crotch momentarily and then I down the rest of my champagne. This is moving too fast. But I can't help it. It's too fun.

"Sorry," he says, nearly stepping away.

"Oh, god, don't be!" I grab his arm and tug him back toward me. Through his suit jacket, I can feel his bugling bicep. His eyes shoot to my hand; it's like static electricity but deeper. I feel it in my whole body, a pulse of energy that zooms through me, from the pit of my stomach through my chest, down my arm, and out my fingertips right into him.

I'd be shocked if he didn't feel it too.

Fuck, I'd love to get his clothes off tonight. Not just yet, though, give it a bit more time. But soon. That would really be the icing on the cake. And I'm not just saying that because I baked the damn thing.

I tilt my head to the side and step a little closer to him. "Don't be shy."

Adam smiles, tongue resting in the corner of his mouth. "I don't know if you can tell, but I've been drinking. My filter isn't what it would be if we'd met in different circumstances."

"I don't mind it."

He blinks. Long, dark lashes. I'd love to ruin that pretty face with my lipstick.

"In fact, I think your pun was right on point."

"Oh my god, Eve, buy me a drink first."

I giggle. Both of our drinks are empty. I release him from my grip and start over toward the bar. "Don't mind if I do, *Adam*."

And from over my shoulder, as I walk away, he replies in a low voice, "I don't mind one bit."

Chicago is already becoming my kind of town.

FOUR

KEIFER

"I love this song."

This girl.

"Come dance with me."

This *woman*.

"Please, Adam."

Eve. "Whatever you want."

She smiles, hazel eyes glimmering with excitement. She shoots back her nearly full glass of champagne and then grabs my hand.

As our fingers interlace, I start to feel dizzy. Every small touch from her makes me drunker, drunker than I already am.

I'm not sure how many whiskies I've had or how much champagne she's had, but I bet combined, the alcohol content would be enough to kill an abnormally small horse.

I can think about my liver tomorrow. Tonight, my mind is all on Eve. And she wants to dance.

I don't think much of my dancing skills, but that doesn't matter. Eve's got me taken care of.

She leads me onto the floor, her hips swinging from side to side in a hypnotic motion. "Come here, Adam."

I go to her, take her up in my arms and we start to twine together on the dance floor. We move together like the wind through the trees, a give and take so easy that I want to drunkenly enter us into a dance competition.

She sings along to the song, tossing her blonde hair side to side. So carefree. I adore her.

I wanna be your lover

I wanna be the only one that makes you come running

I push my mouth up to her ear. "Are you trying to send me a message, Eve?"

She laughs loud, head hanging back as I twirl her around. "I swear, I just like the song."

I wanna turn you on, turn you out

All night long, make you shout

"Because I'd be happy to oblige."

"And people call *me* a temptress. You're so bad," she growls.

Maybe I am, but it's her that's making me feel this way. From the moment our eyes locked across the room, something about her called to me, reached into the deepest part of my body and said, *You need her.*

And even if it's for just one night, I have a feeling Eve is going to rock my fucking world.

We've not explicitly agreed to anonymity, just leaned into it. And I love it. Besides, it feels like we're both anonymous here at my brother's wedding. Whether that's because everyone is wrapped up in their own shit or we're all getting too drunk to see straight, I don't know.

But I *will* take advantage of it.

We continue this back and forth, shooting little flirtations at each other, turning in and out of a dance. Eventually, I pull her into my chest and keep her there. I bury my head in her hair, take a deep breath, devour her scent.

Sweet. With a tinge of bitterness at the end. Just like vanilla extract. When we were kids, my brothers told me that I should take a spoonful of it, that it tasted good. Little did I know they were playing a joke on me. They knew that despite its intoxicating smell, it tasted nasty. And as I wept to our mother about how I couldn't get the flavor out of my mouth, they laughed.

Eve is a little bit like this. Although the bitterness to me is that I can only have her for the night. We are just two strangers at a wedding, looking for a good time.

And man, am I dedicated to having a good time with this beautiful woman.

The closer we dance, the more I'm starting to lose my composure. Her breasts slide up against my chest and her hips are starting to wriggle against mine. I can't keep my "snake" (as I so stupidly referred to my dick earlier) from becoming alert.

I try to pull my focus away from how aroused I'm feeling. Try and remember that my dad is somewhere nearby, that my niece and nephew, my little baby sister, are all here somewhere, their impressionable minds alert and watching.

And then, she whispers, "I can feel you…"

All hope is lost from there on out.

There is want in her voice. She can feel me *and* she wants me.

I push my hips closer to hers so she can really feel what she does to me. Eve laughs, her hands falling to my chest, running down it to my waist.

Though the dance floor is a flurry of people moving, enjoying the music, we've stopped completely.

"What do you wanna do?" she murmurs, her lips nearly touching my chin.

I take her hand in mine. Tight. Protective. *Mine.* Even if it *is* just for the night. "Let's get some fresh air, huh?"

Eve nods.

I loop my arm around her waist and drag her out of the ballroom as fast as I can, finding the door out into the conservatory next door where I took the phone call earlier.

Despite the January weather outside, it's warm and humid in here. The air is clear and easy, all the plants around us adding to our charade. Now we really are in the Garden of Eden. Just the two of us, as the story went. With temptation growing with every breath.

But we didn't come in here for fresh air.

I push Eve up against one of the planters at the center of the room that cordons off the pathway from the plants and wrap the back of her head in my hand. With a gentle pull, I incline her head back.

Her lips are the color of raspberries.

"Perfect," I mutter before kissing her with all I have in me.

Immediately, she hums against my mouth in pleasure. There's been so much pent-up energy between the two of us. The flirting, the drinking, the dancing. It's all coming out right now. Right here.

Eve's hands slip under my suit jacket, pulling so hard at my dress shirt that one of the buttons pops off. Fuck, that's the biggest turn on. A woman wanting me beyond rational comprehension. I press my pelvis to hers and whisper in her ear, "I wanna do things to you."

"Please."

I pull up her skirt, letting my hands feel the curves of her thighs and ass. "Oh my god..."

"There's the apple we were talking about."

I chuckle. "You're funny." I can't get enough of her curves, my hands caressing her anywhere and everywhere. "And so fucking sexy."

Eve starts kissing my neck ravenously. My body is going crazy for her. Her teeth start to pull at my skin. She's going to leave a mark. I want her to. "Oh fuck, how are you doing this to me?"

"It's the story, Adam," she murmurs. She locks her arms around me as if she can't hold me close enough. "We were destined to be like this from the beginning."

This night has gone above and beyond my expectations. I knew it would be nice celebrating June and Jarred's wedding. But it wasn't my night, and I mostly wanted to stay out of the way. Then this vixen walks in, out of nowhere, and my body simply has to have her. How did I get so lucky?

"Let me have you tonight."

Eve shrugs off one of the straps of her dress. It falls, revealing the plump mound of her breast. I immediately grab it and my cock jumps. "Do you like what you see?"

"Is that an actual question?" I say through a breathy laugh.

She giggles and hooks a leg around my waist. Slowly, she starts to grind her pelvis against mine.

I whimper, head dropping to her shoulder. "Oh. Oh god."

"You want to be inside me, Adam?"

I growl. I don't even mind that she's calling me by a name that's not my own. Our game, our roleplay is so fucking sexy. "I'll fuck you right here. Right now."

She's about to answer. I can hear the words "do it" right on the tip of her tongue. But the door we came through to escape the madness of the dancefloor starts to creak open.

Eve and I jump apart. She turns away to tuck her breast back into her dress and I try to straighten myself out.

"Look at – what do you think that's called there?" I say, wrapping my arm around her shoulder and pointing up at a huge tree at the center of the conservatory.

"Hm... there must be a plaque around here somewhere."

We pretend to busy ourselves with searching for a plaque while a group walks through the garden. They're all jolly and drunk, pointing out how different plants look like dicks. Once they're out of earshot, Eve and I look at each other.

Suddenly, we're shy. Like we weren't about to fuck in a public place. She smiles bashfully at me and points to her chin. "You've got..."

I touch my face. "What is it?"

"Lipstick."

"Oh... yeah," I laugh and start to rub blindly at my face.

"No, it's everywhere. And your neck."

"Did you give me a hickey, Eve?"

She touches my neck gingerly and I wince. Yep, definitely a hickey there.

"I didn't mean to."

I shake my head. "I don't care." I take her wrist and kiss the inside of her palm.

The awkwardness dissipates. The want remains.

"We probably shouldn't, here," she whispers.

I glance over at the group that's made their way quite a bit down the path. But I'm sure there will be more to come. "You're right."

"I've got a little place not too far away I'm staying in until I find somewhere more permanent. If you want to..."

"Is that even a question?" I ask. "Absolutely. A hundred percent. I..." I lean into her, sliding my arm around the small of her back. "I need to fuck you. I don't care where or how, but it has to happen tonight."

Eve sighs in pleasure. "Then take me home, Adam. Right now. I can't wait a moment longer."

And what kind of man would I be to keep a lady waiting when she's so desperate?

FIVE

DARA

It was hard to keep our hands off each other the whole ride to my apartment, but we were good. Adam already had to focus extra hard to make sure he could drive while drunk in his mammoth pickup truck. We started the ride with me huddled up to his side, but he relegated me toward the far side of the seat. Couldn't distract him with any groping.

I didn't know people drove huge trucks like this in the city. Seems absurd, but right now the revving, heavy motor feels good under me.

For his pretty boy exterior, Adam's a man through and through. The way he handles the roads and darts through traffic. It's just adding to how much I want him.

The inability to touch has built the tension even higher. Resisting is pretty effective foreplay.

"We're almost there. Take a right at the light," I instruct him. My heart beats faster with anticipation.

Though his eyes are focused on the road, I can tell his thoughts are consumed by me. In fact, he tells me as much. "I can't wait to get that dress off of you," he murmurs through clenched teeth, the green light from the traffic stop casting his face in a wan glow.

"Hm, this thing?" I grab the skirt of my dress and start to inch it up my leg, exposing my thigh.

Adam tries to keep his attention rapt on the road in front of him, but he can't resist a little look. "You're going to get us in an accident."

I giggle to myself and then look out the window at the passing buildings. This is my neighborhood for now. A quaint suburb outside of Chicago, right near Rye's house. Wilmette, it's called.

"What's next?"

"My place is right on the corner. Street parking is free."

"Perfect."

Adam speeds faster to the end of the street and I let out a loud laugh. He breaks hard into an empty spot in front of my building, throws the car into park, and pounces on me. He consumes my mouth with his and pushes me down onto the seat. His hands slide under my skirt, trying to make good on his promise.

"If you wanted to fuck me in your car..." I say between kisses, "...you didn't have to drive me home."

Adam grunts. "You're right. Let's do this the right way."

I didn't know there was a "right way" when it came to a one-night stand, but I would much prefer him to take me inside my apartment than in the cab of his truck. Although that sounds like an adventure in and of itself.

"Don't move," he whispers raspily into my ear and then gets out of the truck.

He rounds the truck, throws open my door, and, without warning, picks me up off the seat in a fluid motion, holding me bridal style in his arms. I let out a loud laugh and kick my legs.

"Shh. Don't want to wake the neighbors," he scolds me and then kisses me.

Adam carries me up the stairs and then drops me so I can open the front door. My hands are trembling as I try to press the key in the lock and it doesn't help that he's rubbing his pelvis up against my ass, letting me know how much he wants me and how ready his cock is to be inside me.

As soon as the door is open, I make a break for it, bounding up the stairs.

"Hey! Wait up!"

"Top floor! Come get me!"

As I rush up the stairs, Adam follows speedily. His lack of high heels is an unfair advantage. I glance back over my shoulder as he gains on me and let out a playful, terrified squeal.

On the last set of stairs before my apartment door, he catches me and pushes me up against the wall of the stairwell. I gasp as our eyes lock.

His beautiful green eyes are almost entirely black from how wide his pupils are. He doesn't have to tell me how much he wants me. I know it from just one look. "You trying to get away from me?"

"Trying to make you work for it."

His jaw tightens. "If you keep being bad, we won't make it to your apartment." He presses his hips against mine so tight it almost hurts. *Hurts so good...* "I'll have to fuck you right here in the stairwell."

"You wouldn't."

"You challenging me?"

I give him my sultriest smile, tilting my head back, taunting him. "You *wouldn't*."

That tips him over the edge. In a flash, he throws up the skirt of my dress, grips my lace panties and pulls so hard that they rip. I gasp loudly. He shuts me up with his lips and as he's distracting me up above, he pushes his fingers inside me. I moan into his lips in surprise and pleasure, warmth bubbling through my body.

Adam grabs one of my wrists and pushes it up against the wall, restraining me. But he doesn't have to do that because I am fully under his spell, willing to be his captive audience for whatever he wants to do to me.

As his fingers pump inside me, he pushes his thumb against my clit like it's a button. I squirm and whimper into his mouth.

He draws back only slightly, so I can feel his words on my lips. "Tell me how bad you want me."

"So bad. I want you so bad."

His fingers move faster and my legs start to shake. "Tell me how bad you want to feel me inside you."

"You're killing me, Adam."

"Tell me. *Beg me.*"

"Please, fuck me. I need you inside me. I need you..." my words get quieter and quieter as pleasure builds and my ability to make sense of the moment vanishes.

Before I can come, he removes his hand. I grunt in frustration. Two can play at this game. When he lets up his grip on me, I turn the tables, ripping open the closure on his pants and delving my hand into his underwear.

He doesn't have time to react before I'm running my hand up and down his cock. Adam's head falls back and he curses.

I push my thumb up against the head of his cock and feel a bead of precum at the tip. "You're already leaking, Adam."

He doesn't respond with words, just a sad whine.

"Should I put you in my mouth?"

Adam nods heavily, blond hair falling into his eyes.

I smile and shove him up against the banister of the stairs. He braces himself against it tightly to keep from tipping right over. I sink to my knees and pull his pants down further, letting him free from his constraints. "Mm, look at your beautiful cock." I kiss the tip and then engulf it in my mouth.

"Jesus Christ... oh my god..."

I hum happily as I take him deeper and deeper. As my tongue swishes around him, Adam loses his strength. His knees start to collapse under him.

"Your mouth. Feels so –"

I take him as deep as I can, nearly gagging on him, and he cries out in pleasure.

Slowly, he droops to the stairs, the weight of bliss becoming too heavy until I have to bend all the way to my belly to blow him.

Adam carefully wraps his hand around the back of my head without pressure or force. His touch is tender. "Fuck, Eve... your mouth feels amazing."

I come up for air. He bristles at the feeling of me being gone, but I immediately make up for it by kissing his ruby, wet lips.

Adam cups my face in his hands, sounds of desperation burbling in his mouth. When he pulls away, our eyes meet. For a second, this wildness suspends, and I am immersed in his needy gaze. He runs his hands back through my hair, pushing it out of my face. "You're so beautiful."

Blood rushes to my cheeks. "Oh. Thank you." I pinch his chin gently. "So are you."

Adam's face shifts. And though he says nothing, I understand him. The energy is shifting.

I get up and leave him like a broken-down doll on the

stairs. It's time we do this for real. I go to my front door and unlock it. When it opens, I step inside and give him one last look before disappearing into the dark.

Heavy-footed follow me slowly up the stairs. He appears in the doorway, his silhouette so tall he almost blocks out all the light from the stairwell.

As if he needs an invitation, he waits there.

And I have an invitation for him.

I undo the zipper on the back of my dress as gracefully as I can and then let the straps fall down my arms. The fabric plummets off me like water, leaving me naked in front of him.

Adam sharply inhales. Says nothing. Just stares at me. At my body.

I can't say I've ever felt quite like this, especially not from a man who was a stranger only a couple of hours before. Like I am perfect enough for a man to sacrifice everything for. Isn't that what Eve did to Adam?

Adam takes a step forward, shrugging off his jacket so it too falls on the ground. Then, he untucks his shirt and unbuttons it as he closes in on me. Step by step by step until we are standing only a few inches apart. Untouching.

I'm thankful the apartment is dark. There is nothing special about it. It's furnished by the leasing company and all my stuff is still in suitcases or boxes. Since I'll only be here for the month, there's no need to get comfortable.

I have a feeling, though, if I apologized, Adam would not bat an eye.

There is only us in this moment.

He takes off his button down, revealing his well-built chest. Faint outlines of abs, a dusting of hair across his chest. His biceps that I had admired earlier are just as burly as I expected.

We stand there, looking at each other's nakedness. The only sound in the room is our breathing.

Adam kisses me. Softly this time. The softest he has all night. Like I'm made of delicate porcelain.

I wrap my arms around his neck and pull my naked body close to his. He's so warm.

Adam hoists my legs up over his hips, holding me under my ass, and walks us up against the wall opposite the front door. He jostles his hips up and down, trying to find my entrance until he does, and I let out a small gasp.

The head of his cock burrows inside me and he pauses, pulling back to look me in the eye.

No words. Just action. I nod, overwhelmed with admiration for how kind he's being even in the heat of a moment like this.

And with that permission, Adam pushes himself inside me.

I can't do much, held captive around his body with my feet off the ground. I do not doubt his strength for a second.

Slow, at first, he dips in and out, in and out. At one point, he pops out of me and we both laugh awkwardly. I reach down and guide him back inside me and we lock eyes as he starts to fuck me again.

His cock stretching me feels amazing. All my nerves feel like they're expanding, reaching out to touch and nuzzle one another, creating cascades of warmth through my pelvis.

Adam's breath is growing labored. He pushes his face into my neck and grunts. I cradle his head in my hand and hold him tight right there. He's the only thing in the world to me right now.

We're both shaking, his speed increasing at a rate that is out of his control. My voice trembles out of me, wordless but emotive. If I could speak, I'd tell him how good he feels, how close I am, how much I want him to come inside me.

Come inside me, come inside me.

As soon as I think that, I wonder if he can read my thoughts, because next thing I know, Adam's going faster than humanly possible, thrusting in and out of me like he's trying to get me to break.

And break I will.

I whimper with each breath I take, warmth turning into a scalding heat. I dig my fingernails into his back, unable to get enough of him in my hands.

And that's what sets him off.

He whines, trying to continue his strokes, but it's too late. Adam slams his hand against the wall by my head and lets out a terrifying yelp. I feel his cock burst inside me, coating my walls with his seed.

And I come too. So hard, clenching around him, pulling every last bit of him out.

"Oh my god," I cry out, tears in my eyes. It feels so good, the orgasm like matches setting each other off one by one. It doesn't seem to stop.

Adam holds me in his arms, kissing my face as the release overcomes me. "So beautiful when you come. So perfect."

He carries me over to the Ikea couch and sits down with me on his lap with a huge sigh. He holds me there, rubbing my back, cooing soft words in my ear. I feel him softening inside me, but I'm not ready to let him go.

In the darkness of my little, temporary apartment, we unwind together on the couch. Completely spent. Not knowing what to say next. Maybe he'll be ready for round two, maybe not. It doesn't matter. This was more than enough.

This was everything.

"You think I can stay in the Garden of Eden with you a little bit longer?"

I can feel him hardening again. This man really *is* a man.

My answer comes in the form of a kiss.

You can stay as long as you want. Want to stay forever?

SIX

KEIFER

The mornings are so dark in January. Hopefully that means I won't wake Eve when I leave.

I have to laugh at myself. I don't even know her real name. To me, she'll always be Eve.

My Eve.

I glance over at her as she sleeps. We finally made it to the bed for round three and fell asleep shortly after. Her blonde hair is a mess across the pillow and her makeup is smudged and runny.

She's so beautiful.

I didn't sleep much. Between the adrenaline of sex and the anticipation of my flight later today, my mind has been buzzing.

I still have to fucking pack. Should have known better than to leave it for the day of. Worst comes to worst, I can buy whatever I need. It's California, not the lost city of Atlantis. But still, I need to be ready at least for the week ahead. Once Monday hits, I'm going to be going nonstop trying to soak in as much information as possible while I'm at Jameson Technologies.

I sigh. Even though I have shit to do, it's hard to think about leaving the Garden of Eden. I reach out and tenderly stroke Eve's cheek. She doesn't move a muscle. Must be totally out from all the drinking and the physical activity.

I think about kissing her. Maybe that'll wake her up. Then I can say thank you and goodbye, maybe get another round of something in.

No. That will just make it harder to leave. That's not what this was. Not about emotions or feelings. Just sex.

Although, I have to say, a few times when our eyes locked when I was inside her, I felt something. Deep in the pit of my belly.

It's her hazel eyes that just get me with her matching glimmering smile. Though I don't know her well, I know she's going to make some man really happy someday. He's going to be so fucking lucky to have a beautiful woman who can bake and knows how to have a good time.

I'll shake his hand if I ever meet him. Or I'll punch his face. Because for a second, I wish that man could be me. If only things were different and I was at another place in my life...

With precision, I slink out of the bed as quietly as I can. She doesn't move an inch. I sneak out of the small bedroom and into the living room. Now that I'm not intoxicated and consumed by her, I get a little better picture of the place.

It's small, furnished without much personality, and mostly just boxes and suitcases. Either she just moved in or it's a temporary place.

I tiptoe through the apartment and pick up my various pieces of clothing. My walk of shame. Thankfully, I'll just be going straight to my house in Mayfair and won't have any family to answer to.

As I wade through the carnage of last night, I find her

dress piled on the floor, a pool of emerald. I remember that first moment I saw her, how much I wanted to wrap myself up in her skirt and never leave.

Dreams really do come true.

I pick it up off the ground and grab a hanger out of the front closet. A beautiful garment like that shouldn't be strewn on the ground. I hang it up from the door frame so that she won't think I've stolen it. That would be a weird guy thing to do, and although I'm not planning on seeing Miss Eve again any time soon, or ever, I don't want her memory of me to be tainted.

Once I'm dressed, I start to make my way to the front door, but stop.

It feels wrong to leave things like this. Completely anonymous and thoughtless.

I just had the greatest night of my life with this woman. She deserves to know at least that much.

I wander around the apartment a little longer looking for something to write with. By the window, there's a notepad with a pencil resting on it. I can't help but take a peek. It's a list of different baked goods with notes attached to them.

Lemon squares
Mini fruit tarts
Italian wedding cookies
Donuts???

These must be plans for her bakery. Her writing is charming, scrawled in pretty cursive that she must have practiced.

I tear off a piece of notebook paper and start to write something.

Eve,
Thanks for a great night. Take good care.

Adam

I frown and bunch it up in my hand. I'm not writing her a thank you email, I'm trying to let her know that I'll carry her memory with me. That she's made an impression on me. That me leaving is a crude thing, but a necessity. I grab another sheet of notebook paper.

Eve,

That was amazing. I'll never forget you.

Adam

I crumple that one up too. Stupid. Saccharine. Corny.

One more sheet. That's all I get. I can't come into her house and use up all her precious notebook paper.

I pace around the room for a little bit, trying to think of the right thing to say. But nothing comes. So, I decide this needs no goodbye. It's just a one-night stand. Nothing more. I shove both of my fuckups into my pocket.

I'd love one last look at beautiful Eve, curled up in a fetal position into her pillow, naked underneath the covers. The thought makes me shiver.

Deep breath. Get going. No reason to look back.

I head out of her apartment, keeping my head down, and disappear into the January cold.

I've gotta get to California.

SEVEN

DARA

The bed is cold when I wake up.

I'm alone.

I blink my eyes open and look at the pillow next to me. It's mussed, but there's no sign of him. My Adam.

Then comes the pounding in my head. Fuck, I drank way too much last night and barely had anything to eat. How many glasses of champagne did I have? I try to remember, but I can't count, not when my head is spinning like this.

I reach into my bedside table for the bottle of Advil I always keep on hand. Then, I flop my hand over to try and find my glass of water from the night before last. When I find it, I knock the Advil back with a big gulp of water. Must kick this hangover's ass.

I shiver. A cold January morning. Would have been nice to wake up next to someone.

At the memory of last night, my body sings but my heart falls. I'll never see him again. He didn't leave a note or a phone number.

I could ask Rye about him, but... that's not what this

was. It was the "memory of a lifetime" not a romance to last a lifetime. There's no need to bother her with the details. Besides, she's got a husband, daughter, and brand-new business to worry about. Too much on her plate. She doesn't need me trying to put the pieces together over a one-night stand.

And I don't even know his real name. From the moment we met, we were bound to be strangers. There's something sort of poetic about that.

It was certainly a "welcome to Chicago", I'll say that. The whole city is my oyster. There are probably Adams on every block.

I don't think I'll be able to get his beautiful green eyes out of my head for a while, though.

My head starts to pulse again. I take another Advil for good measure. Then, back to bed.

My work can really start tomorrow.

"What are you going to do once the lease ends on your apartment?"

"Mm. I don't know. Honestly, I've been too busy to think about it."

Rye and I are walking side by side down the main road while she pushes Ivy in the stroller. There's a beautiful view of the lake just to the right and it's an easy distraction from all my worries.

"Well, you can't have much longer there, can you?"

I shake my head. "No. Just two more weeks. But I've been working overtime at the bakery. I'm exhausted." If I'm going to pay off debts on the bakery property, I'm not going to get to sleep until I'm dead.

Rye gives me a scolding glance. "Dara..."

"What?"

"You need a place to live!"

"No, I need a place to *sleep*. There's a difference," I say pointedly. "I'm barely spending any time there anyway. I'll just extend for another month."

"And then a month after that and a month after that and a –"

"Do you have a point by bringing this up, Rye?" I ask with a smirk.

She shrugs. "Well, you're moving here, right? You need to make it your home."

I sigh. "It's hard for me to make anywhere my home anymore."

She reaches out and grabs my hand. They swing between us as we walk. "I know, honey. But you have me here. And my family. You know you're welcome any time. In fact, you've promised you're going to come for Sunday dinner, and you haven't yet."

"I know. I'm sorry. Just been –"

"Busy. I know. But Dara, you've only got one life. You want to look back on it and just remember that you were busy?"

I have to resist responding flippantly. Rye couldn't possibly understand. She grew up with money and then married into even more of it. Anything I've ever wanted in life I've had to work for. For the past few years, all on my own. "It takes a lot of money to open a business, Rye."

"And I told you I'd give you the capital up front if you'd just let Ash and me –"

"Then the bakery would be yours, not mine. Not really."

Rye doesn't respond. We are both silent as we walk the

rest of the way to the playground. I know she doesn't want her family to get in between the two of us, but it's impossible.

Once we get to the playground, Rye lets Ivy out of her stroller. At nearly a year old, she's starting to do that toddling walk. Rye and I both take one of her hands and help her over toward the swings as she trips over herself. Ivy's always a good breaker of tension. Even if a conversation has become weird, her cute little laugh and stumbling can get us right back on track.

"Okay, Ivy. Upsy-daisy!" Rye lifts her into one of the baby swings and starts to push her gently in the swing.

I stand in front of the swing to catch her and swing her back to her mom. As she comes toward me, I lean in with a big smile and kiss her cheek. Ivy squeals and grabs for a lock of my hair. I don't care when she pulls it. She's too adorable, too full of love to get mad at.

"I'm sorry I keep bringing up the shop," Rye finally says after we get in a rhythm of swinging.

"It's fine. I just want to do it on my own."

"I know. I get it. I felt the same way when Ash was trying to get me started."

I flinch. "You know I'm not trying to say you shouldn't have accepted *his* help. He's your husband. It feels different."

"It doesn't have to be," Rye says with a sweet smile. Her maternal side has come through full force ever since Ivy arrived. "I know you don't want help with the store. I won't offer anymore. But..."

"But...?"

Rye's eyes fall to Ivy as she swings back and forth. "Ash owns a lot of property. And he's got a house just sitting on a nice little cul-de-sac in Mayfair. Right next door to one of his sons, actually. You might have met him at the wedding. Keifer?"

I shake my head. "Don't think I got around to it."

She shrugs. "Well, he's gone most of the time anyway on business. But the house next door is empty, and I talked with Ash about it and we think you should stay there until you get on your feet."

I feel warm inside at the offer. A whole house at the end of a cul-de-sac for me? That sounds like a dream come true. I've never been able to imagine being in a place financially stable enough to have my own house. And here Rye is just offering it to me. Why am I letting my pride get in the way when she's offering to be so helpful? "I really don't want to take advantage of you, Rye."

"How could you possibly be taking advantage when I'm offering, Dara? Really!" She catches the swing when it comes to her and coos to Ivy, "Isn't Auntie Dara being a little *proud*, Ivy?"

Ivy laughs and reaches her hands up to her mother's face, squeezing her cheeks.

"I'm not proud, just –"

"Not used to having the support. Don't think I don't see right through all your defense mechanisms, Dara. We're too close for that."

I sigh. "You're right. I know." The two of us have been through a lot together, from the days working at the bakery up in Madison to me harboring her as a runaway when she was trying to hide her pregnancy from Ash before they got together. Now, here we are, after all this. The least I can do is let her help me a little bit. "*Fine*. As long as I'm not being a burden."

"When did I say you were being a burden?! Goodness, you're putting words in my mouth." Rye pulls Ivy out of the swing and tucks her on her hip. "You can come by for Sunday dinner tomorrow night and grab the key."

I roll my eyes. "Ugh. Fine."

"Why are you so resistant?"

"Because you guys have this whole family thing! I've never had that family thing."

Ivy starts reaching for me. She loves my blonde hair. Rye hands her off to me and she tucks her little head onto my shoulder. "Dara, you *have* 'that family thing' now that you're here with me. You can keep bristling against it, but we're all here with open arms. So, you can either get with the program or keep stomping your feet. It's no use trying to resist it."

Ivy strokes a lock of my hair and I smile. "You're a pain in my a-s-s, you know that, right?" I say to Rye.

She smiles devilishly. "I know. That's why you love me." She wraps an arm around my waist. "Come on. Let's go take a turn on the slide, shall we?"

"Sounds good, *Mom*."

Rye smiles and presses her forehead to mine. "Everyone needs a mom, Dara."

We know that fact better than anyone. Thank goodness I have Rye here to be my surrogate mother from time to time, even if she's only five years older than me. Maybe it's time I stop being mad that she's trying to take care of me and let myself be taken care of.

Easier said than done.

Okay, so San Diego in February is not as warm as I'd like it to be, but a balmy sixty is definitely better than frigid temperatures in Chicago. I'm outside as much as possible, whether I'm hiking or going out with my new pals from Jameson Technologies, taking a run down the beach, or simply sitting out on the balcony of my temporary apartment, basking in the sun.

It's only been two weeks, but I've definitely made this place my home. The apartment resembles my house back on the cul-de-sac. Dirty dishes in the sink, socks strewn about from wherever I took them off, an imprint of my face on a throw pillow where I crashed the night before after staying out too late at the club.

I know it's time to grow up a little bit. And seeing Dad and Jarred settle down with their new wives and children has definitely been making me think. But then I remember I'm just twenty-seven. I'll sleep when I'm dead.

This Sunday evening, I've just come in from a run, sweat pouring down the front of my gray shirt, making it a completely different color. I check my smartwatch for the time. Nearly five thirty. There's a slew of texts from my brothers, Dad, and June. Each of them says something to the effect of, *Call us! We're all at dinner missing you!*

I smile. Sunday dinners. That's the one thing I really miss. When we're all together, not consumed by our own personal lives, we can really connect.

Since coming out to California, it's hard to get anyone for more than a couple minutes. June, my best friend, has been consumed with Jarred, Hayden, and Piper since the two of them got together last May. I'm happy for her... but I miss her.

Funny feeling, being surrounded by people and always feeling alone.

I grab a towel and pat the sweat off my face and then pour myself a tall glass of water before Facetiming the last person who texted me, June. I lean over the counter and wait for the call to be picked up.

The Facetime sound plays and June appears with Hayden right on her hip and a smile on her face. "Wait a second, we're going to the couch so we can see you better."

"No problem."

I get a stellar view of the bottom of her chin as she congregates people together into the living room. I can't make out much, just my name from time to time. Then, she props the phone up somewhere to showcase the entire couch and everyone sits down. It's like a sitcom or something. My big, accidental family. We've been growing at an exponential rate. It's almost comical.

On one end, Dad sits on the couch arm next to Rye, who's bouncing Ivy on her knee. My little sister by a long-shot. She's getting so big so fast. Then, next to them is Jarred with Piper on his lap, although she's recently had a growth spurt and looks uncomfortable no matter how she sits. Piper has been obsessed with Ivy since she was born. The two of them are going to be the best of friends.

Wherever Jarred goes, there's June at his side with baby Hayden. I know it hurts Jarred's feelings to say it, but Hayden is June's twin right from their eyes to the shape of their nose. They're so happy together, still looking like they did on their wedding day.

It's starting to gross me out. What kind of brother would I be if it didn't?

And then, at the very end, Oliver is squeezed in. I'll have to text him and apologize for leaving him as the only single man at dinner. He's probably so tired of the baby talk.

"Say hi to Keifer everyone," June says, waving Hayden's little hand for him.

"Hi Uncle Keifer!" Piper shouts out and Ivy blathers right after her, so close to making the right sounds.

I grin. "Hi everybody!"

"How's California?" Dad asks. "You look like you've just stepped out of a sauna."

I grab my towel and dab off my forehead. "Just came in from a run and saw your texts."

"Gosh, that must be so nice. We've had freezing temperatures for the past week straight," Rye complains, leaning on Dad's leg. "We should take a vacation soon."

"Is everything at Jameson going well?" Jarred asks.

I shrug. "It's all fine. Nothing interesting to report outside of company hours. But tell me about what's going on there?"

Conversation flows easily from there. Everyone has an update, no matter how small. Dad gives me a play by play on what's happening at Hawthorn while Oliver talks about how Trevor is going through the wringer since his breakup with Rowan. "I told him to come tonight, but he's embarrassed to come alone, which is ridiculous because he's been coming for years. Now this one girl breaks his heart and –"

"Easy, man." Jarred pats him on the back.

Oliver crosses his arms, red-faced, steam pouring out of his ears. "Let's talk about happier things. Piper can spell her name now."

"Already?!"

Piper nods proudly.

"You have to show me that when I get there, Pipes. I can't wait to see it." Her returning smile fills my soul with warmth.

"It's amazing," June says. "We're really proud of her." She looks at Piper with a tender smile on her face and gives her a kiss on the cheek, making the little girl smile bigger.

"My baby's growing up," Jarred adds, feigning wiping a tear of his face.

Piper laughs. "Daddy, don't cry!"

The conversation goes on like this for a while. They feed me stories about life at home, about the babies and how they're growing (and yes, even though Piper is closing in on five, she'll always be a baby to me), all the adventures they've been having since the wedding.

I wear a smile the whole time, but inside, my heart is cracking a little bit. I wish I was there to experience all of this. In just two weeks, I feel like I've missed a lifetime. And I still have a month and a half to go, stuck in California.

After a good fifteen minutes, the kiddos are getting antsy and it's time to go. Those minutes went by in the blink of an eye.

"Okay, let's say bye to Keifer, huh?" June says, trying to tame Hayden who is starting to squall for a feeding.

Piper leaps out of Jarred's lap and rushes over to the phone. She holds it way too close to her face. "Goodbye,

Uncle Keifer!" She kisses the phone, and I can't help but melt inside all over again for this little treasure of a girl.

"Bye Piper." I pretend to loudly kiss the camera.

She laughs so loud it almost blows out the speaker. "I miss you!"

"I miss you, Pipes."

She kisses the phone with a loud smacking sound again, leaving the camera blurry with her breath. Then, she attempts to rub it off with her little hands. "Here, Ivy. Say goodbye!"

Piper hands off the phone to Ivy, but Rye grabs it first. The image is flustered until it focuses in on Ivy.

"Say buh-bye, Ivy!" Rye encourages her.

Ivy smiles. Ivy's teeth are still growing in, so she's part gum and part teeth and it's so cute. "Buh-buh!" she says, waving her hand.

"Give Uncle Keifer a kiss!" Piper demands.

Ivy follows Piper's instructions, giving the camera a sloppier kiss than Piper's.

These little moments are the ones I cherish. I miss everyone, but I miss the kids the most. The way they express their love so purely is a motivation for me to be a better man.

The phone gets passed back to June and Hayden. "Okay, now my turn."

June walks off away from everyone else. I've been standing in the same position, bent over the granite countertop this whole time. My back is starting to hurt.

"How're you doing?"

"Don't you need to feed your son?" I ask.

June rolls her eyes. "Well, the last I saw you was the wedding before you disappeared, and we haven't gotten to catch up since then."

A memory flashes through my whole body. It's true, I didn't get a chance to say goodbye to anyone because I snuck off with... Eve. It feels strange to remember her that way when I know it's not her real name. I haven't told anyone about it, but I'm getting the feeling they all know I snuck off to do something dirty. "How's newlywed life?"

"Good! I mean, how newlywed can you be with two kids under the age of five?" she says with a dry laugh. "It's great, though. We're... we're very happy."

"Well, you being happy makes me happy."

"Aw. You're such a sap."

I chuckle. June's been my best friend since we were five years old. There's nothing I want more than her happiness. The fact she found it with my brother is both a blessing and a curse. "You guys figure out your honeymoon yet?"

"Yeah, we're waiting for you to come back so we can pawn the kids off on you."

"Oh, joy."

She laughs. "Kidding. We're going to take a quick getaway in May probably."

"A quick getaway? That doesn't sound like honeymoon material to me."

June blushes. "I just can't stand the thought of being away from Hayden and Piper for too long."

I wish I knew that feeling. Being tethered to someone who needs me. I've said it again and again. I'm not ready for that. But more and more I yearn for it. And I do look forward to it.

"Anyway. Tell me about California. I know you're not being a goody-two-shoes out there. So...?"

I laugh. Hayden starts grabbing at June's collarbone. He's getting antsy. "How about you give me a call in the next couple of days and I can give you the whole lowdown?"

"Yes! Please. I need some hot gossip. Just tell me, any girls?"

I shake my head. "I haven't really been trying."

"You only have so much time out there, Keif! Break a heart or two!"

"I know you don't mean that."

June giggles. "You never know. You might meet the one! But you'll have to bring her back to Chicago. We're not letting you move out there."

Not the cliché bullshit... "*Bye*, June."

"Bye, Keif." She waves Hayden's chunky hand. "Bye, Uncle Keifer!" she adds in the voice she saves for him.

I give her one last grin and then hang up the call.

The apartment feels... too quiet. Even though it's by the ocean and there's always activity outside, there's an emptiness here.

I'm alone.

And lately, when I've been alone, my mind goes to Eve.

I shake off the thought and sprawl out on the couch to watch some TV. But no matter how much I try to focus on the show, I can't get her out of my head.

"Goddammit," I mutter in resignation. I reach into my gym shorts and find my dick is already semi-hard.

The only way I can get her out of my mind is remembering her.

NINE

DARA

The bakery I work at always seems to be busy, but I don't mind. The din of customers filtering in and out keeps me focused as I pipe pastel frosting onto cupcakes.

"Dara, where are the snickerdoodles?"

I glance back at my coworker, Jen, a woman in her mid-forties who manages the bakery. She's direct and blunt, but never unfair. And she always has extra shifts to give me. "I just need to put them on a tray. Give me two."

Jen nods, her cat-eye glasses sliding down her nose the slightest bit.

I put down the piping bag, move to the cooling rack of snickerdoodles, and begin moving them onto a tray for the display case. There's always another task around here. Though I'd rather be working at my own bakery with my own recipes, I'm grateful that my tenure at Ella Rose's Cupcakes and More isn't going to feel like a total slog.

There is one problem, though. Sometimes I can get so in a rhythm that I start to zone out. And my mind drifts into fantasy land. The fantasy can range from the opening day of my bakery to the day I win some sort of prestigious award (that's not an if but a when) for my delicious cream puffs.

And... occasionally, it drifts somewhere completely different.

Okay, occasionally is an understatement. Because often, I find myself thinking about Adam.

My Adam.

I remember touching him, kissing him, feeling him inside me. The memories are so potent they feel like waking dreams. Just the mere thought of him and his growling voice can make me wet without doing a fucking thing.

It's becoming a bit of a problem.

He always visits my imagination during the most banal of activities. Like moving cookies onto a tray.

I pause just for a moment and shut my eyes. Let myself fall into a scenario I've thought about several times.

He walks into the bakery. Afternoon. Golden hour. The sun dances through his golden hair. At first, he doesn't see me, looking into the case of pastries for him to choose from. But then I ask, "Can I help you?" and his green eyes snap up, immediately recognizing my voice.

He smiles crookedly. Both surprised and somehow not. "I knew I'd run into you," he'd say.

There's nothing I like more in these fantasies than knowing he's been thinking about me.

We'd get to talking. He'd ask when my shift is over. And for some reason, I'm the only one working. This would never happen in real life as there is always at least someone to work the register and someone else working on baking or decorating, and that's on a slow day.

But it's my fantasy and I can do what I want.

I'm the only one there. And I say provocatively, "Well,

how about now?" And with a sultry little walk, I go to the front door and flip the "open" sign to "closed".

And we both smile at each other because we both know what's about to happen.

The best place for him to fuck me here would be on one of the metal prep tables in the back. Unsanitary in real life, but for a fantasy, oh so sublime. All the utensils shudder with a clang as he pushes me up against it.

The thing I liked most about my night with Adam was the way he vacillated between being gentle and rough. So, in my fantasy, he pushes my front up against the table, lifts up my skirt, and takes me from behind.

The cool metal singes my skin while the heat blooming between us makes me sweat. His every touch is like worship of my body. As he ravages me, he pulls me up into his arms and pushes his lips to my ear. I can hear his ragged breath. I'm close to coming, too fast for it to be reality, but this is my fantasy. And then he whispers...

"Dara? Snickerdoodles?"

Huh?

"Dara!"

I snap out of my fantasy and look over my shoulder. Jen is glaring at me through her cat-eye glasses and her dyed red hair suddenly looks like fire.

"Why are you just standing there? I need the 'doodles!"

"S-sorry!" I hurriedly shove the rest of the cookies onto the tray and walk them over to the counter.

Jen snatches them out of my hands. "That's the third time that's happened this week. Are you feeling alright? You're flushed."

"I am?"

Jen lifts a hand and puts it to my cheek. "You're burning up."

Oh, god. How do I tell my boss I don't have a fever, I'm just horny?

"I want you to go home."

"Jen!"

"Uh-uh. This day and age, we can't afford to be taking risks. Go home."

My heart sinks. It's only a few hours of work, but that's a few hours of pay. And I need it. "But –"

"I'll schedule you overtime this weekend," she cuts me off as if she can read my mind. Like I said, she's firm but fair. "Take off please."

With shoulders hunched, I trudge to the back of the shop and hang up my apron.

My commute home is longer than I'd like, but better than my old place in Wilmette. Rye insisted after giving me the key to the house that I move in as soon as possible. Wasn't too hard since I was still living out of boxes.

The ride on public transportation gives me the time to think. A walk to the Red Line, take the El up to Lawrence, and then a bus ride west until I hit Mayfair. Then a short walk and I'll be home. I'm used to the cold, being from Wisconsin, so I'm well prepared.

Not to mention if I get chilled, I can just picture my fantasy again. Apparently, that warms me right up.

Stupid brain...

As I wait for the train, my phone buzzes. I'm hoping it's a text from someone, *anyone*, but no such luck.

Just a notification from my period tracker.

Wait. My period tracker?

Looks like your period is a few days late.

I frown. No way. My period is *never* late. Besides, I just got it. Didn't I?

The train comes. It's the afternoon rush, which means I'm cramming myself in between students and commuting businesspeople. I huddle into the corner by the door and open the app.

Indeed, according to the calendar, I'm late. Three days. Which isn't a lot but it isn't...nothing.

Holy shit.

We didn't use protection. Adam and me. I hadn't really thought about it in the moment. Things were heated and we ended each other as fast as possible. There wasn't any time to discuss the details like condoms or birth control... which I've been forgetting to take since I moved to Chicago.

I push my phone to my chest, afraid people are ogling my screen like they're cheating off my math test. *Relax, Dara. You don't know until you know. In fact, you're probably just stressing out. And stress can make you late, right?*

I can't seem to get this line of thinking to stick. By the time the train gets to the Lawrence stop, I'm running to the nearest convenience store.

Without thinking, I grab the first test I see. And then another brand just in case. I haven't had a scare since I was twenty, and even then, I hadn't had sex in five months so there was no way I was pregnant. The anxiety that accompanies a scare, though, is overwhelming, creating a brain fog so dense it's hard to see through.

Just get home. Don't stop. Just go home.

I resist any temptation to run into a nearby bathroom to take the test. The bus, luckily, is on time and I'm home in the next half hour.

As a sidebar, the house I've been staying in is perfect. A little two-story home with a slanted roof and window boxes.

Rye's promised she'll plant some flowers in them for me in Spring.

I'm still only partially moved in. The idea of settling there doesn't sit well with me, mostly because it feels like a handout I'm not sure I'm comfortable taking. But the furniture is nice and the house stays warm during the cold winters. Beautiful light streams in through different windows at all hours of the day. It doesn't even feel like I live in the city. It's my own cul-de-sac of paradise.

Right now, though, I am blind to all the elegant details of my Mayfair abode. My brain is repeating over and over, *You're pregnant, you're pregnant, you're pregnant.* And I have to shout back, *We don't know until we know!*

And boy, am I going to know very soon.

The whole process takes twice as long because I'm trembling, but I get it done. And then I wait.

I pace the hall outside the downstairs bathroom, the old wooden floors creaking under my feet. I can't be pregnant. Because if I'm pregnant that means I have to expend energy on making a choice on whether I want to continue being pregnant or not. And I don't have time to think about making a choice, let alone being pregnant and having a baby.

A whole fucking baby! I'm twenty-five! I'm still a baby myself. With debts to pay and dreams to follow.

After counting down the long minutes, I barge into the bathroom, fully convinced I've totally psyched myself out. There's no way that I'm –

Every coherent thought leaves my brain when I see the test.

Pregnant.

There's a smiley face next to the word.

"Wipe that smile off your face," I mutter, picking up the test and narrowing my eyes. There must be a mistake.

So I take every test I purchased. Each one says the exact same thing.

Pregnant. Pregnant. Pregnant.

I'm fucking pregnant.

I need some water.

I go to the kitchen and get a glass from the sink. The water runs and runs and runs. I stand there watching it. How the hell did this happen?

I know the literal mechanics, but how did I *let* this happen? How could I be so foolish?

Classic Dara. When I fuck up, I fuck up royally. And this is no different.

I need to talk to someone. This is one of those moments I wish I still had my mom or my dad. I wouldn't have hesitated for a second to call them. Now, I'm on my own.

Although, not entirely. I remember about a year and a half ago when Rye sought refuge at my apartment when this exact same thing happened to her. She asked me for help.

I need to be humble enough to ask her for help too.

I whip out my phone and slide down to the kitchen floor, pushing the phone up to my ear and praying Rye will answer. She's gotten so hard to reach.

"I need you," I whisper over and over to myself until, miraculously, she picks up.

"Hey Dar! What's up?"

Just the sound of her voice tips me over the edge. I burst into tears.

"Oh my god! Dara! What's wrong?!"

"I'm such an idiot! I'm so stupid, Rye!"

I hear some mumbling in the background. She's probably telling Ash it's me on the phone. God, he can't know.

That would be way too much. "Honey, tell me what's going on."

"I'm... I'm..." I need someone else to know. I can't shoulder the burden of knowing by myself. "I'm pregnant, Rye."

She pauses for a long moment. Then: "I'm coming over."

When Rye arrives at the house, she lets herself in and finds me still crumpled on the kitchen floor, still weeping.

The first thing she does is fill the water glass I put out on the counter. She hands it to me and sits on the floor beside me. "Here, honey. Drink this."

I follow her instruction, drinking the whole glass in one go. Rye rubs my back.

"Better?"

I nod.

"Now. Tell me everything."

I take a deep breath. There isn't much to tell. It wouldn't even be a novella. "One-night stand. At the wedding. I was so drunk. It was so stupid."

"Stop being so mean to yourself."

I chew on my lower lip. "God, it was just... no protection. No anything. My birth control's just been sitting in my purse. I keep forgetting to take it. I took four tests and – Rye, I don't even know his name. What kind of person gets pregnant by a man she doesn't even know the name of?"

"Plenty of people, Dara."

Through all of this, she's smiling softly. As if she knows plenty better than me. Which she does, I suppose.

"Do you remember what he looks like?"

"I don't know. I had so much to drink." I can't trust my memory. The only picture I have of him is in my imagination, and surely, I've made him into much more of a stallion than he actually is. Drunk goggles will do that to a person.

"Okay, we won't worry about him for now," Rye says. She knows all about that. After Ash got her pregnant, she barely wanted to mention the guy. "I know you're in shock and you've just found out. But do you know what you want to do yet?"

"I can't have a baby..." But I know I want one. Someday. What if this is that day? "But I don't know if I can just..." I can't even say the words. I shake my head. "I can't. Not without considering how that would make me feel." I fold my hands over my eyes. "God, I sound crazy."

Rye pulls me in closer to her. "Not even a little bit, Dara. I know the feeling."

"It's different, though! You were in love with Ash! You knew he was the father! I'm just a sl—"

"Don't you dare say that about my best friend," she says warningly.

I bite back on the self-slander. "I don't know. I'm so tired. I was shaking the whole way home. I'm still shaking."

She grabs one of my hands. "Okay, well, you don't have to make any decisions tonight."

"I'll have to make it eventually."

"If it happened the night of the wedding, you're only about three weeks along. There's plenty of time."

I sigh. "I just want to decide. Shouldn't I?"

"Not tonight! Because tonight, it's just me and you. I'll order food, we'll watch a movie, and —"

"What about Ivy?"

Rye shrugs. "Ash has got her tonight."

"Please tell me you didn't tell him."

"Of course not. I just said you needed me and he understood. He knows what that's like, especially with the boys. The number of times he's run off the past few months to give Jarred some parenting peptalks, he owes me *at least* one night. And it helps you're just a short drive away. Not all the way in Madison. So, what are you craving, *mama*?"

I groan. "Please don't call me that."

"Sorry, sorry, sensitive subject." Rye kisses the side of my head. "Just know that whatever you decide, whenever you decide, I've got your back. Whatever you need. Just like you had mine."

"*Have* yours."

"Yes. Have."

And since the night is entirely ours, we don't get up for a long while. I rest my head on Rye's shoulder and she holds me close.

If I can't have my mom, Rye is the next best thing.

TEN
KEIFER

Sweet Home Chicago. Just at the tail end of March. Thankfully, I missed all the cold snaps and hot flashes March can bring and now, we're headed into April showers.

As I walk through O'Hare, I'm still serving California. Aviator sunglasses, my shirt unbuttoned a little too low, and a tan I hope lasts a couple of weeks.

I hit up baggage claim, and then find my driver who is holding a little sign with the name Hawthorn on it. We always have the same guys picking us up, and today, it's Tim. Tim's classic Chicago Irish and still wears a suitcoat and cap when he drives us around even though other drivers choose to dress down.

"How was your trip, Mr. Hawthorn?" he asks, helping me with the bags out to the car.

"Just great, thanks, Tim. Although, I'm happy to be back." I take in a deep breath of smoggy Chicago air. "Ah, that's the stuff."

He laughs. "You're the only one I know refreshed by pollution, Mr. Hawthorn."

Tim also insists on calling me by my formal name while he prefers to be called just Tim.

"It's not pollution. It's the smell of home!"

He grins. "Well, you're not there quite yet. Hop in."

I climb into the backseat of the car. Plush leather interior and tortoise shell accents. The seat is luxury compared to the airplane seat. First class hasn't been immune to airline greed. Feels like every time I fly, my knees are an inch closer to the seat in front of me. "How fast are we going today, boss?" I ask.

Tim looks back at me from the front seat, a mischievous gleam in his eye. "How fast do you want to go, Mr. Hawthorn?"

What the rest of my family doesn't know is that Tim is an experienced drag racer on the weekends. One time, my plane landed in the middle of the night and Tim showed me his stuff on the deserted highway.

Let's just say, my heart was pumping so hard I didn't sleep that night.

"As fast as legally possible."

Tim rolls his eyes. "You're no fun today."

I laugh and enjoy the smooth ride out to Mayfair.

When we turn onto the cul-de-sac, I'm relieved to see my house is still standing. I always get the irrational fear I've left the coffee pot on, or something disaster-inducing.

However, my relief turns to confusion when I see there's a light on in the front window of the house next door. *What the hell? No one lives there. Unless...* I text the family group chat.

> Someone squatting in the house next door
> to mine?

I stare at the screen, hoping for an immediate text back,

but no such luck. The only logical explanation to me is that someone saw the house is open and somehow broke in. Or… probably more likely, Dad's rented the place. Which I've explicitly told him not to do.

"Are you alright?"

I look up. Tim is looking at me in the rearview mirror and the car is at a standstill. "Oh yeah. Sorry. Didn't realize we'd stopped."

As we get out of the car and grab the bags, I can't help staring at the house, trying to catch a glimpse of anyone inside.

No such a luck.

Eventually, all my bags are out of the car. I've refused Tim's offer of helping me bring them inside; I know he has back problems and the last thing I need is for him to slip a disk hauling one of my suitcases up the front stairs.

He drives off and we exchange a wave. But I don't bring my bags inside.

I need to figure out who my new neighbor is.

I ascend the stairs of the house next door and ring the doorbell.

A few moments pass. Nothing. I knock.

"Just a second!"

A woman's voice. Sweet and warm sounding. Young. I run a hand back through my hair and straighten out my airplane rumpled suit jacket. Want to at least make a good impression.

I hear the door unlocking and take a step back in order to give the resident some space. The door swings open.

My jaw has never hit the ground so fast.

It's her. My Eve. In the flesh. I never thought I'd see her again. And certainly not under these circumstances. She's wearing an oversized sweatshirt and leggings, blonde hair in luscious waves over her shoulders. Her hazel eyes burn in mine.

"Adam?" she cries out, in just as much shock as me.

"Eve?" My surprise turns to anger. "W-what are you doing here?"

"I live here. What are *you* doing here?"

I point at my house. "I live *there*."

She looks next door and then back at me, her wide eyes somehow growing wider.

"Are you stalking me or something?" I ask with vitriol.

Eve's head jolts back and she shakes her head. "Am I what?"

"It's just funny that a woman I had a one-night stand with is suddenly living next door to me. A little fucking convenient, wouldn't you say?"

Her hand is on the door. I can sense she might slam it in my face if I'm not careful, but I can't help it. My temper is inflamed beyond control. "I'm not stalking you. Do you think you're that important?"

I hold back a curse word or two. *You don't know me or where I've come from, Eve.* "How do you have access to this house?"

"My friend's husband owns it."

I frown. Friend's husband? "Rye? You know Rye?"

"Yes. She's my best friend. She offered for me to stay here while I get my work off the ground."

Jesus Christ.

"You must be Ash's son, then, I take it?"

"Did she tell you that?"

Eve crosses her arms over her chest and nods.

How have we fallen so far? Every memory I have of her is... perfect. Now it seems like we hate each other.

"Um. Yeah. I'm Keifer."

"Dara."

Dara. I have heard that name before. In passing. I hold out my hand to hers despite the fact I'm still furious. "Nice to meet you."

"Nice to meet you too. For real this time."

As her hand envelops mine, I nearly shiver. I get hit with the memory of every nasty thing we did. Nearly fucking in the garden, the blowjob on the stairs, having her against the wall with a primal desperation I hadn't known in... well, ever.

I never thought I'd see her again.

That was a part of the thrill.

But now, here she is.

And she's my *fucking next-door neighbor.*

Thank god I'm wearing this chunky sweatshirt. Otherwise, I'd be panicking even more than I already am.

I never thought that if we saw each other again, he'd be so... angry.

His light green eyes are vibrating still from shock.

Stalking him? He really thought I'd stalk him? Do I give off stalker vibes? That's a low blow.

Adam's – I mean, *Keifer's* hand retreats from mine suddenly. "You didn't tell her, did you?"

"What?"

"That we..." He points between the two of us.

"How could I have done that? I didn't even know you were who you are!" I scoff.

He clears his throat and smooths out the front of his button down. "Well, I don't know. You could be lying."

"Oh my god! I am not stalking you! This is all just – it's a–"

"Really crazy coincidence?" he asks with a raised eyebrow.

I don't need this from him. Not after everything I've

been through the past five weeks. I start to close the door. "Believe me or don't. That's on you."

"Wait, wait, wait–" Keifer slams his hand up against the door to keep me from shutting it. Suddenly, the look on his face has melted from frustration to something more tender. I'm pulled back into the memory of what it was like to make love to him. Feeling him inside me.

If only he knew what that frivolous little night has caused.

I never thought I'd be face to face with my baby's father. And I certainly never thought it'd be...

Oh god.

He's Ash's son.

Guess I'm very nearly a Hawthorn now. *Fuck.*

"Sorry, I let my temper get the best of me."

"I'd say so."

Keifer looks away and then rolls his eyes up to me. This guy must be a lady-killer with that look. "Forgive me?"

I hesitate. I'll make him wait for it. "Forgiven."

Then, he smiles. Fuck, that smile. It does things to me. Makes my stomach flip, although maybe that's just the nausea. "You just surprised me. I never thought I'd see you again."

"Me either." He didn't leave a note or anything. It's clear what he thinks about me.

"Listen, I'm really used to having this little cul-de-sac to myself. I was thinking about buying my dad out on this property and doing some construction to make a compound to rival Kennebunkport," he pauses with a small laugh. Perhaps that's a reference only rich people would understand because I'm lost. "Anyway, how about I buy you out?"

I frown. "What?"

"How long are you staying here? A month? Two? Do you have a yearlong lease? I can make it worth your while."

I swallow. "We didn't put terms on this agreement. Rye's letting me stay because I'm trying to get my business started."

"Right. You're the baker."

"Nice memory."

Keifer's eyes narrow. *Yeesh, tough crowd.* "Let me buy you out. Fifty grand. That's enough to get you started somewhere nice."

Is this guy serious? Fifty grand just to get me to leave the house? That's... wow. That's a really nice offer. And I do entertain it for a moment. After all, I could put some money down on the debt, set some aside for the bakery startup costs, and then allocate the rest to renting somewhere else.

But financial means doesn't always pay for the mental energy. What he doesn't know is that I've got more than just buns in the oven at the bakery. And while I'm still not a hundred percent sure if I'm keeping it, it's heavy on my mind at all times. A move would just make things worse. "Sorry, but no."

Keifer's eyes bug out. "No?"

"No. I... I like it here."

"Okay, you're really not selling me on the whole 'not a stalker' thing."

"Oh my god! This is ridiculous."

"*You're* ridiculous! Turning down fifty grand just to go find another apartment? Some people would kill for that money."

My emotions roll inside me like thunder. It's been starting to happen like that, these split-second jabs of anger or sadness. The mood swings. "Well, sorry, I'm not one of those people."

His lips curl up in anger, trying to find the right response, but instead he just growls. Not a sexy growl like the night we spent together, but a growl of abject frustration and loathing.

"Listen, maybe we can talk this all over a cup of coffee?" *You can't drink coffee, remember?* "Or tea?"

Keifer laughs disdainfully. "No. I won't be coming in for a cup of tea." Then, he turns on his heel and leaves me standing in the front door.

A crisp April breeze wafts over me. I don't know what to say. My jaw hangs open. So much I never would have thought was possible just happened.

The original shock and almost glee I felt at seeing Adam-Keifer has completely disintegrated.

That guy is a grade-A asshole and I'm sorry I ever fucked him.

Even more sorry that I'm pregnant with his spawn.

I shut the door and lean back against it. I push my hand up under my sweatshirt and run my hand over my belly. Eight weeks pregnant. That's what the doctor said a few days ago when I went for my first appointment.

People say that during first pregnancies, it can take a long time to show, sometimes as late as five months. But I can already feel my stomach has changed. Maybe I'm tricking myself into thinking it, or maybe I'm just noticing because it's my body and I can feel the minute shifts of it.

This is going to be a hard secret to keep.

Especially with him living right next door.

So, I need to come up with a plan.

I make my way upstairs to my bedroom, pausing in the bathroom because I forgot to take my prenatals this morning. I might not be sure I want this baby, but at the very least, I'm preparing for the possibility.

Then, to the bedroom where I start tearing my closet apart. Rye dropped off some maternity wear that's sitting in a box, but none of that is going to work. It's all formfitting, for a woman who is proud and excited to show off she's pregnant.

Me? I need to do everything in my power to conceal it.

I take stock of all my sweatshirts and sweatpants, big T-shirts, flowy dresses. Anything that I could wear and get away with hiding a pregnant belly. There might come a point that that's impossible, but I'm not thinking that far in the future. All I'm thinking about is right fucking now.

Until my hand lands on the dress I wore to June and Jarred's wedding. The emerald green fabric, wrapped in a drycleaner's bag, hanging there Innocently.

This dress changed my life. I'm not quite sure yet if it's for the better.

"I can't wait to get that dress off of you..."

No! *Focus, Dara.* Keifer is not Adam. While they may be the same person at their core, they're completely different.

That's what I have to say to keep me safe.

Adam is a memory. A fantasy.

And so is Eve.

TWELVE

KEIFER

My alarm goes off at three A.M. on the dot.

Perfect. Just as I planned.

Being the youngest of three boys gives you a certain set of skills. I can be the butt of a joke without blinking an eye, used to be the smallest (until I got taller than Jarred; he can suck it), and, most important of all, how to be very fucking annoying.

I played nice with Dara that first day. Okay, not as nice as I could have been, but nice enough to offer to buy her out of her stay at Casa de Hawthorn.

After she said no, I had no other option.

Plan B is being annoying as hell.

I let her get comfortable for a week. That way, when I put my plan into action, she'd be totally shocked. Plus, I needed to make plans.

There hasn't been anyone living in that house as long as I've been living in this one. And that's the way I've liked it. Solitude can feel so rare in the city. Even when you have money, there are people as far as the eye can see.

Not to mention the person staying there is a woman I thought I'd never see again.

It's not that I wouldn't sleep with her again. But these circumstances make that completely impossible. The second I get even the notion that a woman is following me or creeping on even my LinkedIn page, I'm *out*.

That's just the way I am. It keeps me safe.

Anyways, three A.M.. I leap out of bed and turn on all the lights in the house. Every single one.

Then, I head down to the living room, turn on the surround sound and blast heavy metal at the loudest I can possibly stand it. And of course, I turn up the bass so it rattles the windows.

Speaking of windows, I open all of them. It's a chilly April night, but it's a sacrifice I'm willing to make.

Then, I go into the kitchen, grab a bag of chips and wait.

And wait.

And wait.

Ten minutes go by. Then, a pounding on the front door. *Perfect.*

I amble through the house, slow as molasses. She can wait.

The pounding comes again.

"Just a second!" I call out in a feminine voice, echoing her sentiment the very first day I came back to the cul-de-sac.

When I open the door, I find Miss Dara standing there looking...

Fuck, she looks so cute. Not just cute. Sexy.

Her hair is musty and slept in and she has a sleep mask sitting on her forehead. Her eyes are narrowed with sleep, and she's wrapped in a huge fleece robe. Peeking out from the hem of the robe are bunny slippers.

Why is it when women look their messiest, I want them the most?

You've got a job to do, Keif. Focus.

"Can I help you?"

Dara screws her face together in frustration and gestures into the house. "Your music."

"What about it?" I say with a mouthful of chips.

"It's the middle of the night."

"I wanted to listen to some music. Sue me."

She looks at me like I've got two-heads. She pissed.

I love it.

"You're kidding, right?"

"Listen, old habits die hard. I've been living alone on the cul-de-sac for a long time now. Cut me some slack."

"Okay." She crosses her arms. "I'll cut you some slack this time."

"Cool."

I lean on the doorframe and eat my chips. We stare at each other. I can feel her attacking me with her gaze. "Aren't you going to go turn it off?"

I shrug. "In a minute."

Dara's lips curl to the side. I'm ready for her to spew every curse word she knows at me. But instead, she forces herself into the house, down the hall, and into the living room.

This girl's got nerve.

I follow swiftly behind her and make it just in time to see her unplugging my sound system. Abruptly, the screaming stops.

"Hey! I was listening to that."

She stomps back over toward me. "Turn that on again and I'm calling the cops."

"You wouldn't."

"I would."

Her breath is heaving, just like it was when we were in bed together. *Shit*. She's never going to leave my head, is she?

I tilt my head to the side. "Have you given my offer any more thought?"

"What? Your fifty thousand dollars?"

I nod, giving her a little smile.

Dara pauses and looks me up and down. Feels like she's devouring me with her eyes. I could jump out of my skin. "Dream on, Hawthorn."

"*Hawthorn*, huh?" I have to admit, that's kind of cute. "What about you, Dara? What's your last name?"

"I'm not telling you that."

"Come on, it's only fair for our rivalry that I know."

"Is that what this is? A rivalry?"

I nod. "Seems that way."

Dara sighs. "And to think I was looking forward to whoever moved in next door so they could taste test my recipes."

She tries to get past me.

"Whoa, whoa, whoa, just because we're rivals doesn't mean I can't be your taste tester."

Dara snorts. "It most certainly does."

"Come on! I'd give you honest, constructive feedback."

Dara rolls her eyes, snatches the bag of chips out of my hand, and then strolls back down the hallway to the front door.

I'm too stunned to fight for my chips back. I watch her go, hips swinging in her little fleece robe. Before she leaves through the front door, she turns back. "Palmer. Dara Palmer."

The corner of my mouth turns slightly up. *Dara Palmer.*

My Eve. My temptress. Now, my annoying next-door neighbor. "Palmer, huh?"

She nods.

"Let the rivalry commence, Palmer."

Dara lifts her chin. "It's on, Hawthorn." She puts a chip in her mouth, the crunch so loud it's like she's eating right next to my ear. She eats it, not looking away from me. Her eyes are either fucking me or saying "fuck you", I can't tell which. Dara swallows loud. "If you turn that music back on, I'm calling dispatch. Don't be an asshole."

Then, she slips back out the front door and into the night. I watch from the front window as she hustles back into her house, almost completely dark except for the light over the front door.

I sigh. "Sorry, Palmer. But an asshole is *exactly* what I'm going to be."

Then, I plug the speakers back in and turn up the music.

"I'm telling you, Rye, he's a demon." I am stumbling through the house, trying to find my other shoe.

"I just can't believe it."

"Oh, believe it! Music in the middle of the night, toilet paper in the trees, ding dong ditching? How old is this guy? Seven?!" In the span of three weeks, he's made my life a living hell.

Rye sighs on the other end. I can hear Ivy fussing. She's been having a bit of a hard time with a bad flu and Rye's been having to attend to that on top of all the stuff with her growing flower shop. "I'm so sorry. I had no idea he'd be so immature about this. If you want, I can talk to Ash and have him sort it out."

I grunt, finally finding the shoe. "No. Don't do that. He'd just call me a tattletale." I couldn't imagine his dad getting involved. That would just be embarrassing for all of us. Rye's too shy to talk to Keifer herself about his behavior. Their dynamic is not like that, even if she is technically his stepmom. I glance out the front window and see Keifer hurrying down the sidewalk to his truck as if he's got a fire under his ass. "It's fine. I can put up with a fucking asshole."

"Maybe if you told him that you were expecting, he'd –"

"No!" I shout almost too eagerly. "I mean… no. I don't know. I still haven't settled on an answer for that."

Rye sighs. "I understand, but –"

"Do *not* say anything." I can only imagine the fucking fire and brimstone that would fall upon me from Keifer Hawthorn were he to find out that I was pregnant from anyone but me. He's no idiot. He can put two and two together.

"I won't. Of course, I won't."

I finish tying up my shoe.

"Are you doing okay, otherwise?"

"Otherwise? No. I'm exhausted. I'm on my feet all day and I overslept this morning so now I'm late to the bakery and I can't afford to be late to the bakery because if I'm late, I –"

"Hold up, hon, you're talking way too fast."

I sigh and grab my bag from the front hall. "I'm just tired."

"You're just pregnant."

I close my eyes together tightly. "That too." Although I still can't really believe it. My doctor's been calling me to schedule a follow-up, and every time I remind myself to call back, I just end up forgetting.

"You have to take it easy, Dara."

I take a deep breath. "You're right." I know she's right. Am I going to do anything about that? Hell no. I have money to make, especially if I'm going to be a single mom and ever get my debts paid off.

"And if anything else comes up, I will take care of it, okay? Any messes Keifer makes, you let me know and I'll –"

"Please, Rye, you can't keep cleaning up my messes."

She pauses. I can tell she wants to push back, but Ivy interrupts, fussing again. Louder this time. "Hey, Dara, can I call you back? I have to –"

"Don't sweat it. I have to get to work anyways."

We say our goodbyes and hang up. Rye will do anything she can for me. The operative word being *can*. She's still a mother, a wife, a business owner. Her load is already so heavy. Why should I make her worry with my own shit too?

I take a deep breath and straighten out my big T-shirt and long cardigan that I'm wearing over some yoga pants. Pants that are starting to tighten just the slightest bit. I run my hand over my bump. Closing in on three months. I've got to make a decision soon.

Perhaps me *not* making a decision is decision enough. It's like I'm waiting until it's too late. Until there's a point of no return. And then I have to have this baby.

I've resisted daydreaming about the baby. But now that I'm pausing to think about it and can feel the ever-so-slight curve, a smile pops onto my lips. "Hey... baby." Feels weird to say. But nice. "Don't think I've forgotten about you. Mama's just busy."

Mama. That's sounds right. I haven't said that word in a long time. My own mama's gone from this world. I think about her constantly, but I don't have someone to call mama anymore. Except for me.

Maybe I have to do this.

Shake it off, Dara. You're late for work.

I take a deep breath and greet the day with a smile on my lips. Take a step out onto the front stoop, go down the steps, and –

I step on something slippery. My feet nearly fly out

from under me, but I latch onto the banister just in time so I don't fall. "Holy shit!"

I gather my balance and then look down at the stairs.

Each one is covered in a pool of blue paint. Bright, robin's egg blue paint. My shoes are now covered in blue.

Keifer. Of course, he's responsible for this. Now he's resorting to potentially injuring me? That's low, even for him.

I carefully climb down the rest of the steps. Once I'm on the ground, I back away to take the image in.

My poor beautiful white steps are now ugly, bright blue. I nearly burst into tears. Arguably, that's an over-reaction.

Arguably. I am pregnant after all.

God, if I had fallen, I could have…

I shake off the thought. That settles it. if the thought of losing the baby ricochets through my body painfully, then there's no way I'm choosing to get rid of it.

I touch my stomach again and narrow my eyes. "This means war."

I took the day off from work. I've been working doubles and overtime for weeks, so Jen was thrilled to be able to give me a day off. Not that I can really afford it in the long term, but I can't help myself.

Luckily, there's a shed in the backyard with all the things one needs to take care of a house. Including paint-brushes.

My day goes from a workday to a project day. I take a paintbrush and go to town with spreading out the paint Keifer left on my front stoop so that the stoop becomes entirely blue. Shockingly, he didn't leave enough paint, so I have to hit up Ace Hardware to get some more.

To be doubly sure I know what shade I need, I go to the back alley and check his garbage cans. Bingo. Three cans of blue paint complete with a shade name and label.

Keifer has no idea who he's screwing with. I'm thorough. I'm detailed. And I don't give up. Comes with being a baker. Always tinkering with recipes, making sure they're perfect, never backing down when something comes out not quite the way I want it. Maybe he doesn't think much of me, but he ought to start.

I purchase several more cans of paint. Because we're the only two houses on the cul-de-sac, we may as well match, right?

After I'm done with my porch, I start to work on his. I work on it into the evening, so when he pulls onto the cul-de-sac, I'm on my hands and knees painting his last step.

Keifer parks his mammoth, gas-guzzling truck and steps out. Shocked. I always seem to shock him. At least I can count on that. "What the hell are you doing?"

"Painting. What does it look like?"

"No, no. It looks like you're painting."

I start brushing the front of the step gingerly. "I figured since you made my stoop look so nice, I ought to do the same for you!" I say with a cheery grin.

"Oh. Well. You're so welcome for that. I thought blue would look nice."

"Yes, it's such a perfect shade."

We are both quiet. Assholes can't stand when you make lemonade out of lemons. So, here I am. Making things look nice. I stand up and dust off the front of my pants that are now speckled with blue paint. "Well, I think I'm all done. I'll need to seal it tomorrow, but –"

"No, you've done more than enough, Dara. Thank you."

He looks so mad. I've come to love that look. It comes out every time I've foiled his plan or given him something to be annoyed by. After all, the reason he's doing all of this is to get rid of me. He'd like nothing more than for me to cut bait and run.

I'm not going to do that.

"Really, Keifer, I want to make sure this stays for a very, very long time."

"I'm sure you do."

I pick up the last can of paint, half full, but enough to cause some damage, and go toward him. "Do you not like it?"

"What makes you think that?" he asks, his lips thinning into a line.

"I don't know, you're frowning a little bit." I point to his forehead. "Right between your eyebrows."

Keifer touches his forehead, and as he's distracted, I pretend to trip. The can heaves forward and blue paint coats the front of Keifer's beautifully pressed, expensive work clothes.

He gasps. "What the fuck!"

"Oops. Sorry."

"You did that on purpose!"

I'm not interested in playing this game anymore. "Yeah, well, so did you when you poured it on my front steps!"

"I didn't pour it *on you!*" he shouts, kicking off his shoes as fast as possible. However, they are already victims of the attack of blue paint. "Fuck, these are Ferragamo!"

"No, you didn't, but I nearly wiped out from slipping on the fucking paint! You could have seriously hurt me!" *And your baby.* I toss the paint can at his chest. His reflexes are fast, and he catches it. "Jackass."

I turn on my heel and head into my house.

This was so fucking worth skipping a day of work. I'm going to treat myself to some takeout tonight.

"Dara!" Keifer shouts out right before I make it inside.

"What?!"

The moment goes silent except for the sounds of the city in twilight. Birds have returned from their southern vacations and people drive on neighboring streets, coming home from their days at work.

It's almost comical, me on my blue steps, him in front of his. So ridiculous and foolish looking, it almost seems purposeful.

Keifer's anger has melted into something resembling... is that *embarrassment*? He bows his head slightly, looking up at me with his light green eyes. "I'm sorry. It was never my intention to hurt you."

I don't care if he didn't mean it. He should have thought about that. And consequently, there's no reason for me to accept his apology. "Sure it wasn't," I mumble and then barge into my house, slamming the door behind me.

The next day, when I leave for work, my steps are blue. When I'm back, they're white. However, the splotches of blue remain on the grass, on the sidewalk, everywhere else but the steps.

I'm a little annoyed, but I also wonder if it's a peace offering from Keifer.

Fat chance. Damage has been done ten times over. It's clear he wants nothing to do with me, would go as far as to hurt me, even if it was an accident.

What kind of father would he be? If he's willing to hurt

me like this? Granted, he doesn't know, but I think he doesn't even deserve the chance. Not if he is willing to go this far to throw me out and keep me out of his life.

As I unlock the front door, I stop suddenly. Right in front of the threshold, to the right, there is a small blue splotch. I bend down to look at it. It's a small circle with a line sticking out of it. The longer I look, the more it looks like an apple. Or maybe it's just a blob? I can't tell. But if it is an apple, is he trying to reference our night together? The Garden of Eden? The temptation that he now so obviously regrets?

Regardless, it must have been purposeful. I'm sure Keifer spared no expense for the painters to do a rush job like this.

Maybe he left it for me.

As much as I try to forget about it, the blue apple haunts my thoughts the rest of the day.

I make my way down the sidewalk to the front of Dara's house, two cartons of eggs in my arms. I'm running out of ideas, okay? It's been five weeks, just over a month, since I've returned, and Dara isn't showing any signs of budging. I've done every trick I can. I've been severely limited since the paint debacle when Dara told me she almost hurt herself. That was low, even for me.

The point isn't to hurt her or to scare her. It never was. I just want to annoy the shit out of her. I have to admit, though, the goal has become less about getting her to leave and more about seeing her adorable looks of annoyance. Hearing her huffing and angrily grunting when she realizes I've done something silly.

She looks like an angry doll in her big shift dresses and cozy sweatshirts that dwarf her size. I know how tiny she is, I've had her in my arms. It's interesting in her day-to-day life how much she hides her beautiful body.

I digress. It's hard not to with Dara around.

The fact of the matter stands: I want her gone. I've been

unsettled ever since I got back home. A weird feeling in the pit of my stomach that something just isn't right.

She's not showing any stalking behavior necessarily. But one has to wonder when a woman they fucked and left in the middle of the night becomes their next-door neighbor.

Anyway, it's go time. I lob an egg at the front window of Dara's house. The yolk and white drip down the glass. The May sun shines down on it, causing the slimy liquid to sparkle. Perfect. I throw a couple more across the façade of the house. I feel like I'm twelve years old, grinning ear to ear at being an asshole.

I remember that I'm twenty-seven. Maybe I shouldn't be so pleased with myself.

Once the first carton is done, I toss it to the side and start on the second. In the second-floor window, I get a flash of Dara's hair. Shit. She's coming. I heave the rest of the container toward the house so eggs splatter all over the front stoop and sprint down the side of her house to hide.

I hear the front door open and then her adorable little growl. "Keifer!"

I cover my mouth to keep from laughing.

"What the hell is wrong with you?! Argh!"

I peek around the side of the house and watch her stomp down the steps and tear off in my direction. She hasn't seen me. Not yet. But she's on a mission. I sprint down the side of the house, past the hose, and to the back where I can hide again.

Her fists are clenched at her sides and she wears a sweatshirt with the UW Madison Badger on it that goes down to her mid-thigh. She grabs the hose with the spray nozzle attachment and turns the water on.

Oh, Dara... you're making it too easy for me.

Dara pulls the hose laboriously back toward the front of

the house and I tiptoe behind her until I reach the spigot. As soon as I know she's far enough away, I turn the spigot down to almost nothing. I hear her curse.

"You've got to be kidding me."

We do the cat and mouse routine again, her running off down the side of the house and me hiding at the back so she can check on the spigot.

"I swear to god, Keifer, if you're still fucking with me, I'm going to scream," she yells.

I bury my mouth in the collar of my shirt. I can't help it. This is hilarious.

Then, she's off to the front of the house again. So, of course, I'm going to turn down the water.

This time, she lets out a curdled cry. "What the hell is wrong with this thing!"

I rush down the side of the house and watch her as she unscrews the spray nozzle and looks right into the barrel of the hose.

Jackpot.

As fast as my legs will carry me, I run to the spigot and turn the water. All. The way. Up.

That's when Dara screams bloody murder. I sneak down the side of the house and have to hold in a guffaw. Dara is a fucking sight, soaked to the bone and dripping from head to toe. Her mouth is hanging open, a shock from the cold water.

I think I might have just pushed her right over the edge.

Dara suddenly looks right at me. Shit. I've blown my cover. Her eyes are nearly black from how wide her pupils are. Does that usually happen when you're mad? Her jaw is clenched tight, baring her teeth to me. "I'm going to *kill you!*"

Oh shit.

I make a break for it down the side of the house and start to climb the fence, but when I turn around, she's not following me. Where'd she go?

I continue scaling the fence and leap into my yard, cautiously creeping toward the back door. She didn't just disappear into thin air. She must be planning *something*.

I make it to the back door and right inside my house. Unscathed.

That is, until I see the trail of water on the ground. She's here. In my house. *Fucking psycho.*

"Dara? I know you're in here..."

I tiptoe deeper into the house. The path of water is messy and scattered about. I'm not sure where she could be.

"You're a fucking asshole."

I turn around on my heel. Dara is standing there, dripping with water, hanging off of her own skeleton, shivering. "You're fucking crazy. For coming into my house."

"I'm crazy? You're the one who is obsessed with me."

"You think I'm obsessed with you?" I scoff, taking a few steps toward her.

"You won't leave me alone! You basically spend your every waking moment trying to make me miserable. If you think that's because you hate me, you're sorely mistaken." Her anger dissipates into a smooth smile. "You're *obsessed*."

I pause before replying. I'm not obsessed with her. I want her gone. There's a difference there, isn't it? So what if I like the added benefit of her reactions? And that I like looking at her? And from time to time I remember our night together with more fondness than I probably should? I'm only human, dammit.

"I wouldn't be doing all of this if you would just leave."

She crosses her arms and leans into her hip. "Not happening."

I take a couple more steps toward her, the gap inching closed. I tower over her. "Then you're obsessed with me too."

"Fuck you, Keifer. I had no idea that I was going to be your next-door neighbor. It's funny that you think you're important enough to be in my every waking thought. Because you're not."

"Really?"

"Really."

"You don't ever think about us?" It just spills out of my mouth without thinking. But now that it's out there, I'd love to know.

I need to know.

Dara sputters for a second. Her cheeks go red.

I smirk. "You do.

"N-no."

"Oh, come on. Of course, you do."

Dara tightens her lips together and then slaps her hands up against my chest. I'm expecting her to push me away, but instead, she latches onto my shirt and pulls me into her, lips slamming into mine.

My body blooms with heat. Every one of my nerves buzzes with the memory of being consumed with Dara.

With Eve.

The kiss is so intense, she knocks me off balance, pulling us back into the open doorway of the kitchen until I have her pressed up against the counter. She breaks the kiss and whispers raggedly, "I hate you."

"I hate you too," I murmur back and then kiss her, my tongue delving into her mouth.

Hate and love are not opposites. That much is obvious from the way we melt toward each other, our anger making way to a passion I haven't ever known. I rake my hands through her dampened hair. Though she's frigid and wet, there is only heat between us.

I'm already hard, pulsing my hips against her. Dara spreads her hands out against my back and then slides them down to my ass, pulling me tightly against her. She wants me. I can feel it.

"I hate you so much," she says against my mouth.

"Let me show you how much I hate you."

Dara turns around to face the counter and grinds her ass against my cock.

"Fuuuuck."

"Don't act like you don't want me."

I forcefully push myself against her and she gasps. I push my mouth against her ear and growl. "You want my cock?"

Dara nods with a whimper.

"You hate me so much that you want my cock?"

"Goddammit, Keifer, just fuck me."

She's so fucking desperate for me. And I'm desperate for her. My cock is throbbing so hard in my pants. How is she doing this to me? What special thing does Dara Palmer have that my body craves so bad?

I run my hands up her thighs, under her sweatshirt, grab onto her little bike shorts and pull them down to her knees.

Dara shivers. Her body's broken out into goosebumps. As much as I hate her, I want to take care of her. I don't want her to be cold or in pain. I want to make her feel amazing and hear her screaming my name so loud it shakes the whole house.

"Don't tease me. Just do it."

"Whatever you say."

I don't waste any time teasing her clit with my fingers or

admiring her wetness. Just as Dara demanded, I plunge my cock into her. So warm. So tight. Just like I remember.

She throws her head back with a moan.

"For hating me so much, you certainly make nice sounds for me." I chuckle in her ear. I start to run my hands up from her thighs to her hips and just as I'm about to reach for her belly, Dara snatches my wrists and pins my hands to the kitchen counter. She pushes her hips back against me, taking my cock deeper. I gasp. "Shit. Oh my god."

"Stop wasting time being a smartass and *fuck me*."

I hesitate for just a microscopic moment as my eyes catch hers. She is wild. It's something I saw in her when we met all those months ago, but there's something different now. It's deeper. More primal. From her gut.

This woman needs me to fuck her.

And despite our preexisting relationship, I'm more than ready to oblige.

I thrust my hips into her, gaining speed as I go. Pleasure building between us like trying to build a fire. We exchange breaths and moans with each passing moment. Fuck, I fit so nicely into her. And she takes me so well, often wriggling her hips around me to take me as deep as she can.

I drop my forehead to her shoulder and start to curse. Her hands remain on mine so my palms are pressed to the counter. "I want to touch you, Dara."

"Can't."

"Let me, please."

"You haven't earned it."

That sets me off. I'm going to fuck her so good that I *earn* the right to touch her. Every part of her. I can get back to that perfect night in January again. I know I can.

However, I have to be patient.

And unfortunately, my body doesn't work well with patience.

Stroke after stroke, I get closer and closer to coming.

"I'm about to come, Dara, I'm about to –"

Before I can finish, Dara screams. I'd be worried about her if I couldn't feel why. Her pussy clenches around me so tight it feels like she'll never let me go.

"Holy shit, holy shit, holy –"

I come with her, deep inside. Euphoria spills into every corner of my body, an orgasm so powerful it shakes the house. Just as I'd hoped.

Dara's fingers curl between mine. Our clasped hands rest on the counter as we both try to catch our breath.

I kiss her temple softly. I can't help it. Even if we hate each other, I still want to care for her.

"That was good," she says and then nudges me back away from her.

I could stay buried in her pussy the whole day, but the woman wants what she wants. I slide out of her, immediately wishing for her warmth again. I tuck myself back in my pants and wipe my sweated forehead with the back of my hand.

Dara pulls her shorts back up, but not before I see my cum dripping out of her.

Fuck, not again without the condom.

"I'll buy you Plan B."

Dara turns, wide-eyed. "Huh?"

"For the..." I gesture to her general lower body. "Unless you're on something."

She looks askance. Her mouth opens and closes like a fish, and then she nods. "Yeah. Yeah, sounds good. Thank you."

"Least I can do."

We stand there awkwardly. Drenched girl and rude boy.

"Sorry about the eggs and the hose."

"Yeah. You should be."

Ouch. "I'll clean it up."

Dara runs her hands back through her hair and then straightens out her sweatshirt. "Thanks."

Silence. Her hazel eyes meet mine.

"You can egg my house and spray me with water. You can wake me up in the middle of the night with loud music and rev your truck at five A.M.. But no matter what you do, *I'm not leaving.*"

Without another word, she pushes past me, shoulder hitting my arm. Her footsteps come with dripping water all the way to the front door. I don't move a muscle until I hear it close behind her.

I have no reason to question her. I can tell she means it when she says she's not leaving. No amount of my pranks or shitty attitude will change that.

But if these pranks make her mad like *that?* I want more.

I'll do whatever it takes to get Dara to hate my guts.

"Okay, this is it! What do you think?"

I walk into the empty storefront with a smile on my face. It's dingy and in need of paint and furniture, new light fixtures, everything that would make a business worth going to. But it's a blank canvas. "It's perfect."

"I knew you'd like it," Rye says with a smile, sidling up to me. She's wearing her usual work attire: hair pinned back, pen behind her ear, and a green apron with shears in the front pocket. "And it helps that I'm right next door."

"Thank you. This was... more than generous." Ash and Rye put up all the capital to get a hold of the building right next door to her flower shop. I tried to ask them not to, but they refused.

"You're my business partner. It's just business."

I smile and take a quick walk around the perimeter of the main room. "It's going to be a lot of money to get this all shaped up," I say with a sigh.

"And you know that won't be a problem," Rye replies in a sing-song voice, crossing her arms.

I roll my eyes. She's always so eager to throw money at the problem.

"What do you think about having it open in time for the new year?" she asks.

"The new year? That's going to be next to impossible. So much has to get done. The interior has to be rehabbed, I have to finish up making the menu, and I'm... you know..." I gesture to my midsection. "Preggers."

Rye waves her hand. "We'll get people to do all the behind-the-scenes stuff. All you have to focus on is the baking."

"Well, eventually, I'll be too tired to be on my feet, you know?"

"Trust me, I remember. Just think about it. It would be a huge grand opening and it'd be just in time for people planning their weddings in the summer and fall."

I nod. That *is* the perfect time of year. "If you're going to put any money into it, I insist on paying you back."

"I hate when we talk about money," Rye sighs. "It's always so hard with you."

"Well, I'm sorry, Miss Moneybags. Not everyone is married to a billionaire. Some people want to do things ourselves."

Rye's eyebrows jump.

Fuck, that was a low blow. "I mean..." I shake my head. "Sorry. I don't know why I said that."

"You're not wrong. Money makes things easier."

"I know, but I don't mean to say you're not talented. You know I don't think that. You could have gotten it done on your own."

Rye shakes her head. "Not this fast. Not to the scale I'm already working at."

At least she's aware of how much privilege her money gives her.

"That's all I'm trying to do, Dara. It's not that I don't think you can't do it on your own. I'm just trying to give you that same confidence and oomph I got to start off. You know? I know how long this has been your dream."

It's true. Rye and I met several years ago back in Madison when we were still young and unafraid. We've gone through each other's dreams with a fine tooth comb trying to figure out all the steps that it would take to get there. Our biggest dream of all would be running a flower shop and bakery in tandem that could do events together.

We're so close to that. So why am I pushing it away when she has the funds to make it happen?

I sigh. "I don't know why it's so hard for me to accept handouts."

"They're not handouts! It's people who believe in you saying, 'Hey, we want to help because you're amazing!'"

I shake my head. "Let's talk about something else. I'm getting a migraine from this conversation."

Rye nods. "I know you're going through a lot right now. I don't mean to add stress."

I touch my stomach gently. "Yeah, my emotions are all over the place."

"How are things at home? Is Keifer still being an ass? Because if he is, I'll –"

I let out a loud laugh. "Rye, it's fine! I can handle him."

"You can't afford *more* stress. Not good for the baby."

I haven't told Rye about my new "arrangement" with Keifer. That would just make things more complicated. Plus, she doesn't even know that he's my baby daddy. I wouldn't know where to start *that* conversation.

I never thought I'd enjoy Keifer pranking me. But for

the past week and a half, I've been craving it. Because now, after every stupid little thing he does, I get laid.

I know I'm playing with fire. After all, I'm growing much faster than I'd like.

I just can't stop.

Not only is Keifer Hawthorn a divine fucking lover, but my hormones are raging nonstop. I am *hungry* for sex. I crave it.

Thank god my next-door neighbor is so eager to please.

Even if he is an asshole in the process.

"I'll be fine. You have to trust me, *Mom*."

Rye blushes. "I'm sorry."

"It's okay."

We stand in silence, looking at the bakery-to-be.

"I'm glad you're keeping it," Rye says softly.

I shoot her a look of surprise.

"The baby."

"What makes you say that?"

Rye's eyes grow glassy. "Because you deserve to be happy, and nothing's made me happier in my life than being a mom."

I try to smile, but feel tears in my eyes too. I grab Rye's hand and squeeze it. And I tell myself for the one millionth time that *I'm not alone.*

Maybe one day, I'll actually believe it.

———

"God, you're a fucking asshole."

"I love it when you call me that."

We're in the midst of another post-practical joke session right in the front hall of his house. I'm on top of him, riding him like there's no tomorrow. There's an overturned blueberry pie on the ground to our left. Somehow, Keifer switched out all my sugar for salt and I didn't even fucking notice while I baked an entire blueberry pie from scratch. As soon as I took a bite, I stomped over here, demanded he open the door, and threw it right on the ground before giving him a piece of my mind.

This man is on every one of my nerves, and I love it.

Keifer holds tight to my thighs as I bounce on his cock. Feels so good stretching me from this angle. I play with my clit as I move faster and faster. I roll my head around with a moan as a wave of pleasure tumbles through my body.

"You like that?"

"Shut *up*."

The tension between us is always thick and rife. I love being mean to him. It turns us both on way more than it should.

I ride faster and faster until I can barely remain upright. I put my hands on the ground on either side of his head and ram my hips on him over and over.

"Don't hurt yourself."

"I said 'shut up', Hawthorn."

Keifer locks his arms around my waist. I don't push him off. It's innocent enough. Besides, I'm wearing a loose shift dress that hangs over my front so loosely that it'd be impossible to make out my curves. I'm probably being overly cautious.

"God, your tits."

They're bigger. "No touching."

Keifer moans. "I know. You're so cruel."

I start to laugh, but I'm cut off as I find a way to our ending. My body tenses up, heat building and building until I'm hit with a wall of orgasm.

Keifer follows soon after, coming deep inside.

He doesn't know that it's alright he's doing this, which is why I have two unopened boxes of Plan B back at my house. I don't doubt he'll offer to buy me another one after this session.

I roll off of him without lingering in post-coital closeness. We lay side by side, breathing heavily.

"Fuck, Palmer. I like you on top."

"Yeah?"

"Yeah, you're a fucking machine."

I laugh. Even though I despise him, I still love his compliments. I love knowing that he likes fucking me enough to keep coming back and playing our game. "Thanks, I guess."

Keifer rolls onto his side to face me. I remain on my back, staring at the ceiling. I never stay for too long after. It's an in and out in the most literal sense. "Hey," he whispers.

"Hm?"

He doesn't respond.

I glance over at him with a frown. "What's up?"

Keifer takes a deep breath and then asks, "Why won't you let me touch you?"

I clam up for a second. "Because I hate you."

He chuckles, face reddening. "Actually, though." His hand shifts toward me. I can feel the threat of his touch. My skin crawls.

The truth is, I'd love for him to touch me. I remember how full of adoration his touch was. How perfect and devotional.

I miss it.

But if he touched me, then he might know.

And I can't afford that. Not yet. Maybe not ever.

"Um... I've gained weight," I finally say. "And I'm really self-conscious about it."

"Is that why you're wearing all these loose dresses and baggie sweatshirts?"

"You got a problem with my dresses and sweatshirts, Hawthorn?"

Keifer smiles. "No, not at all. But I have a problem with you not knowing how beautiful you are. Regardless of any weight you've gained or... yeah."

I stare at him. Why's he being so nice to me?

"I just think you're beautiful, Palmer."

I swallow and can't even manage a thank you before I'm up on my feet. "Sorry about the pie. Although you deserved it for the whole salt thing."

Keifer doesn't get up, just looks at me. His eyes are trying to determine if he's done something wrong. "Yeah, I did."

"Anyway, see ya." I rush out of the house and back to mine without looking back. But even once I'm in my own house, my heart doesn't stop racing. Keifer is always just a few steps away. Right next door. He worships my body. Wants to touch me. Thinks I'm beautiful.

It doesn't matter that he's been a jerk to me all these weeks. Because I want him so bad.

I'm starting to want him more than just physically. I want him in a way where he can say that I'm beautiful and it doesn't terrify me.

That, however, would require telling him the truth. Being so utterly vulnerable it might make me sick.

And with that thought, I'm off to the bathroom to quell a wave of nausea that's just cropped up.

I remake the pie, this time with sugar, as pies are usually made. And once it's out of the oven, it's perfect. Sweet and tart at the same time, berries macerated to perfection, crust the perfect balance of crip and buttery.

This will definitely be on the menu. Everyone needs a classic pie at a bakery.

After having a piece of my own—and a piece for the baby too, I'm not a monster—I stare at the pie for a moment.

This might be a decision I regret. But I have no one else to share it with.

I cut a few pieces and put them on a plate which I then wrap in plastic. I quietly go out of my house, walk the few feet to Keifer's and raise my hand to ring the doorbell.

I can't bear to face him. This isn't what our relationship is.

I put the plate down in front of the door, ring the bell, and then scurry back to my house with only seconds to spare before he arrives.

I watch him from one of the windows as he steps out onto the front stoop, sees the plate, and then smiles.

That smile... I want to bottle it and keep it forever.

Maybe he doesn't hate me. Maybe he just doesn't know what to do with me.

SIXTEEN

KEIFER

This might be my best prank yet.

I've jerry-rigged a huge wire spider over the front door to descend on Dara right when she opens it. I dug it out of the garage from a box labeled "Halloween Decorations." Lately, I've been trying to get more creative with the pranks. It seems the more ridiculous, the more fired up Dara gets, which is great news for me.

I'm embarrassed to admit I think about her all the time. She's starting to haunt my every waking thought. While I'm at work, I zone out trying to come up with ways to terrorize her so she'll run right into my arms, punish me with her body. Sometimes, people call me out for it. On more than one occasion, Oliver's had to clap in front of my face to snap me out of my trance.

Everyone at Hawthorn right now, though, is distracted. Jarred and Dad are both consumed with life at home, kept busy with their little ones, and Oliver is always on alert to help Trevor through a tough moment post-breakup.

Thank god I'm unattached. Just seems like unnecessary stress. I'm already thinking about maybe heading off on a vacation for a month this summer and working remotely. Get away from the constant frazzled nerves of parents of young children and the drama of breakups.

Who needs that?

I'm waiting right outside Dara's house to watch it all play out before I go to work. I know she usually heads out to the bakery just after me and I don't want to miss this.

I lean up against my truck, arms crossed, smug smile on my face. Waiting.

Sure enough, just a few minutes later, Dara opens the door, setting off the mechanism that releases the huge wire spider right in front of her face. Her eyes widen and her jaw drops.

I start laughing with abandon, not afraid if she knows it's me. If I'm lucky, she'll push me into the truck bed and fuck me silly. "Oh my god, you should see your face!"

Dara is silent. Her body wavers.

Oh shit. Not again. I know when people are about to faint. I had to take June to the hospital for fainting. That's when we found out she was pregnant with Jarred's son. What a mess that was...

Her eyes start to roll back. Have I seriously scared her that badly?

"No, no, no! Wait a second!" I leap into action and rush up the stairs, catching her in my arms before she can collapse all the way to the ground. "Palmer! It's okay, it's fake! It's not real!"

She's out cold.

I shake her. "Palmer! Dara! Hey! It's okay." I touch her cheek and tap it gently. "Can you hear me? Dara?"

Her eyes flutter halfway open. "What's going on?"

"Dara! Dara, I'm so sorry I scared you. You passed out,

but it's okay, because you're..." I trail off. Dara is pale and her skin is cold. "We have to get you to the hospital."

I pace outside Dara's hospital room door for what feels like a lifetime. I can't believe I pushed her this far. I wouldn't be surprised if she never wanted to talk to me again after that stunt I just pulled.

Why won't you just grow up, Keifer?

Perhaps I've never gotten over being the youngest child. Always a baby, even in my twenties. Perhaps it's time I get a grip and start playing into that.

The door opens suddenly and the doctor, a friendly-faced older woman with a bobbed haircut, emerges.

I hop to attention. "Hey, doc, is she alright?"

"You're the husband, then?"

I blush. I had to tell them we were married so I could be here when Dara wakes up. "Yes. That's me."

She smiles kindly. "She's just fine. She's asleep right now."

I heave a sigh of relief. "Thank god."

"This is very common given her condition. But it's good you brought her in, especially since she was out for a few seconds."

I blink. Shit, does Dara have some illness I don't know about? And now I've just forced myself into her private life because I was an asshole who wanted to see her screaming about a fake spider?

Might be time for a therapy appointment to work out my issues, Christ.

The doctor touches my wrist gently. "I can tell you're worried. But everything's alright. I promise. She just needs more fluids and you need to make sure she's eating enough. It can be hard if she's nauseous, but she needs to have enough calories to support both herself and the baby."

Baby. The word hits me like a ton of bricks.

Dara's pregnant?

I think *I'm* starting to feel faint now. I need to sit.

"Especially now that she's nearly at the halfway point, her body's going to be working overtime."

My mouths goes dry. *Halfway*. That means about four and a half months. I start doing math in my head. That puts the date of conception right at the end of January. Right when we had our one fantasy night together. Adam and Eve in the Garden of Eden.

Dara's baby is mine.

I shake off my shock. Just have to get through this interaction and then I can process everything. "Right, of course. Thank you, doctor. I'll make sure that she's taking care of herself."

The doctor smiles. "And may I offer you congratulations."

I smile back despite the turmoil in my head. "Thank you."

"Best job I've ever had is being a parent. Enjoy it." Finally, she leaves me alone to process the atom bomb that's just exploded my life as I know it.

I stumble over to a chair against the wall and collapse.

Four and a half months is a long time. She must have known, right? That would be a long time not to know.

And if she knew and she's been hiding it from me...

And I've been a fucking asshole to her. The woman carrying my child.

I push my hands over my eyes and try to breathe. My thoughts are moving so fast I can barely make sense of them.

How did I go the way of Dad and Jarred without even blinking an eye? What's wrong with us?

I've always wanted to be a dad. I just thought I had more time. I *do* have more time. Just because she's pregnant doesn't mean I have to revolve my life around this baby.

Something must be wrong with me that I'm valuing my freedom more than creating life in this world. I know I'm young, but I never thought I was a coward. Faced with the reality, though, I realize that I'm not as brave as I thought I was.

I'm terrified.

The fact remains, however. She didn't even tell me about it. Clearly, she isn't *interested* in me being a part of this baby's life. Or hers, for that matter.

If she wanted to tell me, she would have. So, if she didn't tell me, she doesn't want me to know. And I'll have to behave as such.

I look at the door to Dara's hospital room. I can't just abandon her. I'd like to know if she's okay. But I'm afraid that as soon as her pretty hazel eyes land in mine, I'm going to lose it and start asking questions.

I need backup.

I pull out my phone and call Rye.

"What?!" she shouts loudly as soon as I tell her what's happened.

"I'm at the hospital with her now."

"Is this because of your stupid pranks? Because I swear to god —"

I didn't know Dara had told Rye about the pranks. They're best friends. I guess I should have assumed. But for Rye not to say anything... that must have been Dara's wish. "It was my fault. I'm... sorry."

Rye huffs. She's never directed her anger at me, or any

of us boys, for that matter. Guess there's a first time for everything. "Don't apologize to *me*."

"You're right."

I can hear her footsteps as she rushes around. "I'm coming now. Don't move."

"Okay."

She hangs up on me before I can say goodbye. I drop my phone into my lap and rub my eyes. I'm such an idiot. I'm such a selfish kid.

Dara's child deserves better than me.

Finally, I get the nerve to go into the room. I creep inside quietly. Dara is asleep, looking like Sleeping Beauty ripped right from the cartoon. Her blonde hair puffs out on the pillow around her face and her lips are blushed. She's regained her color.

My eyes travel down her frame to her midsection. I focus hard on it. Either my eyes are playing tricks on me or there is the slightest change in her figure. The smallest swell.

That's why she wears the baggie clothes. It's why she won't let me touch her.

Still in shock, I go to the chair beside her bed and sit. Her palm is upturned at her side and as much as I'd like to slip my hand into hers, I resist.

Dara has kept me at a distance. And that's where I'll remain.

I blink my eyes open. The ceiling is sterile. Fissured tiles you only see in stores and schools and...

I take a deep breath. The air is sour.

The hospital. I'm in the hospital.

I backtrack. I remember the doctor talking with me as I was nodding off, the ride in Keifer's truck where he made me lay in the back with my legs up so the blood went to my head, the look in his eyes when I was in his arms...

That stupid spider.

Shit.

This is not good.

My hand moves reflexively to my stomach. The doctor said the baby was fine and that fainting can be common for some women. But that was still terrifying.

"Hey."

I jerk my hand away when I hear his voice and turn to see Keifer. I can't believe he's here with me. "H-hey."

"How are you feeling?" he asks in a small voice I've never known to come from him. His eyes look everywhere but my own.

"Tired. Okay, though."

He is quiet, sucking on his lower lip.

"You didn't have to stay."

"I... of course, I did. It's my fault you're here."

I bite back on refuting him. Sure, maybe his spider scared the shit out of me, but the real reason he cannot know. "Thank you," I say. It's touching he felt compelled to stay.

Keifer drops his head and looks at his hands. What's going on with him? It feels like he's not saying something. Although my judgment might not be the best right now. I am recovering from a faint. "Now that you're awake, though, I'm going to go."

My heart falls. "Alright."

"I called Rye, though. She's on her way. Should be here in like fifteen minutes."

At least I won't be alone. I'd like to be here with him, though.

What's happening to me?

"Thank you."

He nods and then gets to his feet. His whole body is collapsed in on itself. Not the tall, cocky Keifer I've come to loathe and enjoy. Perhaps it's the hospital atmosphere. Maybe he has bad memories from the death of his mother.

I know I would.

"Okay, I'll... I'll see you," he says awkwardly and then rushes out the door.

I push myself up onto my elbows and watch the door as it shuts behind him. A sadness creeps over me.

I think I've just lost him.

"Thanks for driving me home."

"Of course! You think I'm going to make you take public transportation home from the hospital? That'd be sadistic," Rye says from the driver's seat as I pop open my door.

Before I get out, I twist around to face Ivy who has been very well-behaved in her car seat. I grab her little foot and shake it. "Bye, Ivy."

Ivy laughs, putting her hands up to her cheeks. My eyes fill with tears. Now that I know for sure I'm going to become a mother, I can't wait for all these moments. I know there's going to be a lot of suffering along the way, but I know it will be worth it.

As if reading my mind, Rye touches my shoulder. "You need to eat better. And take it easy."

"Trying. I'm trying."

"I'm serious. Fainting is no joke, Dara."

I sigh. I'm not willing to get into an argument with her right now. I'm too tired. It feels like our entire relationship has just become her mothering me and knowing better than me. I'm kind of exhausted. "I'll do better. Thank you."

I get out of the car, give my final goodbyes, and make my way up the front stairs of my house as Rye drives off. I stop mid-unlocking my door when I realize the spider is gone. No sign of it.

Keifer must have removed it before I got home. I get a pang of sadness knowing that his pranks have probably come to an end. It's for the best, clearly. But without that tension, it means our physical relationship is probably also at an end.

I look over at his house. The truck isn't in the cul-de-sac.

Everything seems oddly still.

He's probably not home.

Not that it really matters anyway. What would I do? Go

over and thank him again? No, I need to give him time to cool off, release that panic.

I'll stop by tomorrow to properly thank him.

And maybe...

No. I couldn't tell him. Not yet.

But from the way my belly is growing, I'm running out of time for "not yet".

Three days.

Three days and no sign of Keifer. The first day, I went over with freshly made cookies as a token of my thanks and, when he didn't answer, left them on the front porch. The second, I saw that the cookies had been gobbled up and left out front by racoons. Now, this third day, I've been watching his house every moment I get to figure out if he's home.

I don't know why he would want to be on the cul-de-sac by himself. It's been eerily quiet.

I get the feeling he's avoiding me. I tried to casually ask Rye if he might be on a business trip, but she didn't have the information I needed.

On this third day, my worry consumes me. From the outside, I know I look like a crazy person. But this feels like the only way.

I sneak over into his yard and start to peek through windows. The house is in a state as if he disappeared out of thin air with dirty dishes in the sink and a half-drank cup of coffee on a coaster in the living room.

Each place I look, I have a memory of us.

Him fucking me against the kitchen counter... in the front hall... up against the backdoor.

I stare at the burgundy couch and remember how it felt to bury my face into the cushion as Keifer pumped his fingers into my pussy.

Fuck, I can remember it as if it's happening right now.

I press my hand against my groin to try and relieve the pressure of my throbbing clit, but that doesn't help. I'm already wet. This happens now that I'm pregnant. Even the vaguest thought of sex and intimacy gets my clit screaming for release.

"Dammit…"

Though the cul-de-sac has been too quiet and too lonely, there are some advantages.

Like being able to touch yourself while you look into your neighbor's living room.

I slip my hand into the front of my underwear and start to play with myself.

Replaying the memory again.

Keifer's long, thick fingers filling me.

"If you hate me so much, why are you so wet for me?"

He pushes my hair off the back of my neck and kisses the column of my spine. He takes in a deep breath, inhaling me, making sure he gets every last bit of me.

"God, it's annoying how hard you make me."

I laugh. He pushes his fingers deeper in response and I moan.

"Love your sounds. Love them even more when I'm inside."

He removes his fingers, unsheathes his cock, and teases my opening with the head. I take a stuttering breath as he shifts back and forth. Teasing me.

Keifer takes a handful of my hair and twists my head so he can kiss me, but instead, he speaks against my mouth. "Tell me you hate me."

I do.

He smiles. "I don't believe you."

I say it again.

Keifer slides his cock inside me and fucks me hard and fast. I bend over the back of the couch, a ragdoll to his control.

"Are you going to let a man you hate make you come?"

I whimper in affirmation.

Keifer tinkers with my clit as he thrusts into me. I was already so raw from his fingers that my orgasm is right in my grasp.

"I'm going to come inside you."

I gasp.

"I'm going to fill you up."

This isn't how it happened. This isn't what he said.

"I'm going to give you my baby."

My whole-body snaps back to reality. I come, my entire body trembling, fingers soaked from my juices.

In reality, I'm standing outside my neighbor's window staring at his couch and I've just touched myself into orgasm.

God, Dara, why are you so fucking weird?

Shame beating in my face, I rush back into my house and upstairs, leaping right into bed under the covers as if that's the only thing that can protect me from the world.

Why did that feel so good? Why did the memory shift like that?

And why did it turn me on?

I'm already carrying his baby. He can't make me pregnant a second time.

But how wonderful would it have been if we had been able to make it happen *together*? Not by accident. By choice.

Because that's what he wanted. Needed.

Before I know it, I'm crying. I hate to admit it, but I miss him.

I miss his antics and our back and forth. I miss his touch that I'd grown accustomed to almost daily.

I miss Keifer.

If I'm honest with myself, there's always a part of him that will be Adam to me. I know he's locked inside there. Maybe if the circumstances of our meeting again had been different, I would have gotten more of his charm and flirtation than his frustration. If that man came through just a little bit more, I could tell him that a piece of him is already a piece of me.

I wrap my hands around my growing belly. So close to being undeniable.

All I can picture, though, when I imagine telling him the news, is his anger. I've taught myself to crave his anger.

Not anymore.

Family dinner is basically like a daycare at this point. With three children, now there is a constant focus on everything they need and want. Who is having a tantrum? Who is hungry? Who needs a diaper change?

The children are spread out around the table with Ivy in a highchair between Dad and Rye at one end of the table, Piper holding court at the other with Jarred, Oliver, and Trev, and then June balancing Hayden on one leg while she tries to eat her asparagus without him grabbing it off her fork.

The conversations we are having have changed. They are all light and bouncy, with lots of pauses to coo to the babies. Even if Oliver and I were sitting next to each other, we probably would still be sucked into whatever coddling needed to be done.

It's suffocating.

"Keifer? Keif?"

I shake myself out of my trance and look at June beside me. She's got a concerned look on her face. "Hm?"

"You okay?" she asks, shifting Hayden on her lap. He's

gotten exponentially bigger since the wedding, with the biggest chubby cheeks you've ever seen.

"Yeah. I'm fine."

"You sure? You're kind of doing that thing."

"What thing?"

"You know…" She lets her eyes go glassy and stares off across the table with her mouth open like a fish.

"I don't look like that!"

"Yes, you do!" she laughs.

I thwap her on the arm and she does the same to me. To be honest, things haven't been the same since she and Jarred got together and she became a mom. It's not just that she doesn't have time to shoot the shit and fuck around, but she also just has her mind on other things. Though she doesn't actively make me feel this way, I can't help but feel like a child compared to her. She went from single, jobless June to a mother and wife in the blink of an eye.

Although, I guess I've gone to being a father in the blink of an eye. Am I a father if the baby hasn't been born and the baby's mother hasn't told me the baby exists?

"Are you tired?" June asks and softly touches my arm. "We don't have to stay long after dinner."

I've been staying with June and Jarred since Dara's fall. I had rushed home from the hospital, cleaned up the spider, threw all my necessities in a bag, and hopped in my truck without a destination in mind. I needed space. To get out of there and clear my head.

So, I drove in circles. I would start driving up to Wilmette to the family home, but chicken out and then head down to Oliver's pad in the West Loop. Eventually, I settled on Jarred and June's. I really needed to see my best friend. I hadn't had the guts to tell her exactly what was going on, but I knew she wouldn't turn me away.

I told them I just needed to not be alone for a bit. And they took pity on me.

However, after three days, I've realized what I really should have done was take a last-minute flight to Cancun. Because being holed up with the Hawthorn-Reed family has put baby fever on my brain.

Piper has always been the best little kid. And while Hayden is fussy, he's my godson and I feel bonded to him. Of course I'm going to start thinking about what it would be like to have my own.

"There's no rush. Unless you need to get the kids home," I reply and push some food around my plate.

June doesn't respond right away. I can feel her mismatched eyes, one hazel, one dark brown, zeroing in on me. We're not good at lying to each other. At least not for long. "What's going *on*, Keif?"

I glance around the table. Everyone is consumed in some conversation. We could slip away for a few minutes and talk.

If I don't, these thoughts might consume me.

"Come on," I say, jerking my head toward the door. "Let's talk in private."

June frowns. She follows me to the door, dropping Hayden into Jarred's arms on the way. I watch her whisper something in his ear and him glance back at me with bewilderment. She kisses the top of his head and he touches her elbow in such a delicate, casual away that is so intimate I could cry.

I want that with someone. I'm so incredibly jealous watching all this love unfold around me.

June comes to meet me in the doorway and, in silence, I lead her onto the terrace and toward the fire pit down by the lakeside. The days are starting to last longer as May turns into June, but the evenings still have a chill in the air.

June wraps her cardigan more tightly around her. "Are we far enough away that we can talk now?"

"I just wanted things to be private."

"Well, we're definitely out of earshot of the dining room inside, so..." she teases, but when I don't laugh or smile, she touches my shoulder. "I've been worried about you. Tell me what's going on."

I take a deep breath. "I need you to sit down first."

June rolls her eyes. "Alright." She sits at the firepit edge and looks at me.

"Suppose I had a friend. Let's call him... Cheifer."

"Cheifer Gawthorn."

I have to chuckle. She's known me so long she doesn't question when I'm being ridiculous. "Exactly. My friend Cheifer." I start to pace slowly as I explain. "Cheifer was invited to a wedding in January. His brother and his best friend."

June smiles proudly. "I love that I'm a part of this story."

"You're not. It's Cheifer's brother and friend, so shh."

June laughs and leans back.

"Cheifer was flying solo but met a girl at the reception and they snuck away and..." I let the sentence fade away, but I know that's all she needs.

"I knew Cheifer was a manwhore."

"Hey! Don't talk about my friend Cheifer like that!"

"You're right. Sorry. Continue."

I clear my throat. "Cheifer had a one-night stand with this girl."

"Was it good?"

Was it ever. "Yes. Amazing."

"Good."

"Now, he never learned her name. And she didn't learn his. So, they had no way of finding each other after the night."

June twists her lips to the side and narrows her eyes. "And I'm assuming he didn't leave a phone number?"

Ah, shit. "No. No, he didn't."

She reaches out and bats my calf. "Jerk!"

"It was a mistake!" *I know that now.* "Anyway, fast forward, Cheifer finds out that this girl is his new next-door neighbor."

June's eyebrows jump. "Dara?!"

"Shh! Lower your voice!"

"Sorry, but that's your neighbor, right? The girl who came to dinner a couple months ago?"

My jaw drops. "She came to a family dinner?"

"Yeah, while you were out of town. Just one. She brought these amazing macarons. God, they were so good. She's a baker, right?"

I wave my hands to metaphorically clear the air. "We're getting off track. She's his neighbor. And he was a jerk because he's young and foolish and thought maybe she was creeping on him and –"

"Oh, Keifer. Not every woman is a stalker!"

"*—and* he tried to force her to leave by being a jerk but that ended up creating a lot of tension that, uh, needed to be released and –"

She smiles knowingly. "You started fucking her."

I wince. "Yeah, and to make this long, really ridiculous story short, through a series of events that is entirely too complicated to explain, he found out that she's –" I try to finish the story, but the word won't come out.

June waits, hands folded in her lap. "Keif?"

"She's... I've..." I look out at the lake. The sun has nearly set, the water glimmering eagerly. "She's pregnant."

Silence. Water lapping at the retaining wall. I feel June's eyes on me, but I can't look at her. I'm too embarrassed.

"Yours, Keif?"

"Yeah. Yes. But she doesn't know I know. It's..."

"Complicated."

"Right."

June gets to her feet and stands beside me. It's nice not to feel so alone for a second. She squeezes my arm. "You Hawthorn boys all have an M.O., huh?"

"I know, it's so embarrassing!" I moan and put my hands over my face.

"I'm just kidding!" She wraps an arm around me and rubs my shoulder. "Well. How do you feel?"

"I don't know. Confused. Stressed. Angry."

"I think that's all normal."

My shoulders fall. "Why wouldn't she tell me?"

"I have a little bit of expertise on that subject," June says, polishing off her nails on her shirt wryly. "Because she's scared, Keifer. Especially if you were being a jerk like you said you were."

I sigh. "That wasn't about me, that was about Cheifer."

"*Riiiiiight.*"

We look at each other. Despite the stressful circumstances, we both smile.

"So, tell me. What do you want?"

"Like..."

She shrugs. "It's a simple question. What do you want?! You know there's a woman having your baby. How does it make you feel?"

"Great." The answer comes out before I even have time

to process it. It's true, though. "You know I've always wanted to be a dad."

"I know."

June knows all my deepest secrets. My best friend since kindergarten. It's harder as a man to be honest and vocal that you want to be a parent someday. I've never hid that from her, though. "But this feels all wrong."

"Does that mean you don't want to be a part of the baby's life?"

"No, no. I think I do, but she hasn't even told me that she's pregnant, June! She hates my guts."

"Well, you didn't do yourself any favors in that department."

I narrow my eyes. "Not helping."

"Just tell her that you know, Keifer. And if she hates your guts, okay. You don't need to be with her. I said as much to Jarred when we were figuring out what we were going to do. But maybe offering that olive branch that you want to be in your child's life will soften things."

It's strange to be in a position opposite from my father and brother. They both had to make the choice to show up for the women carrying their children. I have to make the choice to show up and convince her that I deserve a chance to make things better.

"Keifer?"

I look at June. Her eyes are swimming with sparkling tears. "What's wrong?"

"Nothing's wrong." She grabs my hands and smiles. "I'm so happy for you. I know how much you want this."

Hearing my desires reflected back at me affirms every thought I've had. I'm going to do my best to show up for Dara. For our baby. We can have our own lives, juggle our hopes and dreams. Her building her bakery, me my career.

And we can do it together. Whether there is love there or not.

At the end of it all, the love I already have for this child will be enough.

I decide that night that it's time for me to head back to the Mayfair house. I get my stuff from Jarred and June's and, in the dark of night, pull onto the cul-de-sac.

The lights are out in Dara's house. It's pretty late after all. I'm glad she's resting. She needs it.

Dara deserves to have someone looking out for her. Regardless of if she wants to build some sort of future with me for our child, I can support her that way. We can be friends. I can take her to appointments and be there for her when our child is born.

If she wants it, of course. Only if she wants.

I head into my house. A sour stench permeates the air. *Fuck, I didn't do the dishes.*

In the morning. I'll get back to stasis first thing in the morning.

For now, though, my bed calls to me.

However, as soon as I'm under the covers, ready for a good night's sleep, my brain is wide awake. Still spiraling out of control with thoughts.

But the thoughts aren't about my impending, possible fatherhood.

They're about Dara.

Beautiful, sexy, wonderful Dara.

The fact she's just a house away makes it worse. I can feel her energy so close to me.

I conjure an image of her naked. I want to know what

she looks like. Her breasts growing heavier with each passing day, her middle growing round with our child. Thinking about Dara changing because of me...

Fuck, that makes me hard.

I try to get my mind off of her by thinking about things I have to do at work tomorrow or about natural disasters and shipwrecks, but my mind keeps going back to her.

The thought of her growing bigger. Being able to touch her. To love her. To fuck her.

Without questioning, I slide my hand into my boxers and start to stroke my cock. *Fuck, it's so sensitive.*

I picture her on top of me, belly round with life, her hands perched right at the top of the mound. Her sweet, sly smile as she looks down at me, teasing my cock with her lower lips.

No wonder she's been so horny and wet. Pregnancy will do that to a woman.

I wonder how insatiable she would really be if she had access to me all the time.

I quicken my pace, faster and faster, my cock growing harder.

I imagine Dara finally choosing to sink down onto my cock, her head falling back and pink mouth opening in pleasure.

How tight she'll be around me.

And the base of her belly grazing my stomach as she starts to move her hips.

"Oh god," I whimper into the pillow. My hips are bucking involuntarily at the mere thought of her naked, pregnant body. If this were happening in real life, I'd probably come in ten seconds flat.

My daydream is so detailed it's like she's moaning right

in my ear. Climbing higher and higher, begging me to go faster, her body so strong and full of life.

Needy beyond compare.

How my hands want to be able to caress her middle as she closes in on an orgasm. How I want to encourage her, tell her how beautiful she is carrying my baby, how much I need her.

"*Shit!*"

My cock spasms hard in my hand, bursting with come into the crotch of my boxers. I'm hit so hard with pleasure I need to gasp for air, my eyes shooting open.

As my body tries to settle down, my cock doesn't seem to relax. He's still semi-hard. Calling to me. *Again, again, again. Touch me again, think about her again.*

I'm totally fucked.

The room that I've deemed my office is a hurricane of papers and books. It reflects how I feel internally. Everything is all over the place and I'm not sure how to tame it all.

I've been working at my desk all morning, trying to plan the expenses for the bakery. All of that hinges on me paying off my debts which I should have all taken care of in three to four months if I keep working at this rate.

But I'm already getting tired. I feel the baby sapping my energy with each passing day. Don't get me wrong, I'm overjoyed that the baby is happy and healthy according to the doctor when I had to be rushed to the hospital. There's just going to come a point where rushing around the bakery with a bump the size of a beach ball and swollen ankles isn't going to be sustainable.

And when the hell am I going to get a chance to clean up the office?

Perhaps having a baby just dooms me to a life of always being messy. If that's the worst thing my life is, then I think that's okay.

I can't shake the feeling though that I'm criminally

unprepared to be a mother in all possible ways. I've been thinking so much about my own mother lately, wishing I could lean on her for advice and help. Rye is great, but it's not my flesh and blood. Not the woman who carried me and can give me advice about when certain milestones happened for her and if I'll ever be able to eat onions again or will they always make me nauseous.

How can I love this baby if I feel so alone? Do I even have enough love to give?

Dara, you're getting distracted. Focus.

However, I'm not able to get back on task before the doorbell rings. It's probably Amazon, in which case I can just leave it and they'll drop it off. I just bought a new bottle of prenatals and some books on the whole *mothering* subject.

Not a minute later, the doorbell rings again, followed by a knock.

"Dara!" a distant, familiar voice shouts. "Are you home?"

I pause. Is that...Keifer? Is he home? I woke up this morning and went straight to the office at the back of the second floor and didn't even think about looking to see if he'd come back.

I leap up from my desk and rush down the stairs to the front door, trying not to look to excited. I can't help it, though. He's back. And I'm relieved I haven't driven him all the way to Timbuktu for being afraid of a spider.

When I open the door, I remember I'm still in my pajamas. *Smooth, Dara. Really fucking smooth.*

But Keifer...he looks like a million bucks in a loose button down and a pair of jeans. It's effortless on him. I'm almost jealous. I'm so taken with his beauty that I nearly don't see the bouquet in his hands. Big, pink peonies.

"I wasn't sure if you were home," he says with a lopsided smile. He pushes the bouquet toward me. "These are for you."

I take them, the peonies' intoxicating scent miraculously not making my stomach flipflop with nausea. "Thank you. They're beautiful."

"They better be. I told Rye to give me the best."

My eyes widen. "Did you tell her you were giving them to me?"

"Well, I told her I owed you an apology. Several, actually. So I don't think she's onto anything that..." he gestures between us to indicate the entanglements we've found ourselves in recently. "Listen, can I come in? I need to talk to you."

I look back into the house. "Things are a little messy, but –"

"I don't mind. This is important. Please?"

I frown. He's never been in my house for a normal reason. A reason not involving anger-fueled sex or a fucking practical joke. But I can tell this isn't a joke. Keifer is adamant. Not forceful, but... there's a firm look in his eyes. He needs to speak with me, and he needs to do it now. "Okay. Come in." We go into the house. "Let me just put these in some water."

Keifer follows me into the kitchen. We are both silent as I fill up a vase, my only one that Rye gave me when I moved in because "Every woman needs at least one vase," according to her, to which I said, "No one's giving me flowers."

I'm grateful I have it now. Once the flowers are in the crystal vase, I put it on the kitchen table and admire them with a soft smile. "They look so nice there. Thank you."

He doesn't respond for a moment. His lips twitch.

"Is it wrong if I say that it's good to see you?" I say softly. Maybe I'll regret it, but it's the honest truth.

Keifer smiles. "No, it's not wrong."

I take a step toward him. "To be honest, I've been missing your stupid jokes. I guess I had started to look forward to them."

"Even though I made you faint?" He chuckles.

"Well, you didn't know I'm severely arachnophobic?"

"Ah. Noted."

I smile and look down. "I was wondering if you were avoiding me."

Keifer hesitates and then sighs. "Dara. I know."

I tilt my head like a dog trying to hear better. "Sorry?"

"I know that you're...pregnant."

My body goes numb. I have one million questions and don't even know where to begin.

"Whoa! Okay, don't faint on me again!"

Before I can even realize what's happening, Keifer slides his arms under mine to keep me from falling. I didn't even notice my knees had given out. I'm in shock. "H-how do you know? Who told you? Did Rye – did Rye?"

"Shhhh...let's sit first."

Keifer helps me into a chair where I sit limply staring at the table in front of me, not even concerned for him to see me cupping the underside of my belly through my bulky sweatshirt. He knows. There's no reason to hide or lie.

I should have known this would come out eventually. I just thought I'd have control over it.

Keifer sits in the spot beside me and faces me, knees nearly brushing mine. "Your doctor thought I was your husband...it was the only way I could go back there with you. And she told me that I shouldn't worry because the baby was fine and...yeah. That's how I found out."

I close my eyes. Maybe if I don't look at him, he'll go away. Maybe this is all a dream.

"I'm sorry, I should have just told you when you woke up, but I was so confused and shocked and –"

"I don't blame you," I croak out.

Keifer slides his hand across the table almost as if he's going to reach out and touch me. He doesn't. "When did you find out?"

"A week before I moved in here."

"So you knew when I came home."

I raise my gaze to his. He doesn't look angry, but his words feel like an attack. "Yes."

"Why didn't you tell me?"

"After you left me without any way of contacting you, I knew you wanted nothing to do with me. And then you came back and for a second..." I was shocked, but it was my Adam. "And then you didn't really give me a lot of faith you would have been kind to me when you realized it was me who had moved in here. I didn't think you deserved to know after you acted like that. Or would even want to."

Keifer's eyebrows jump up. He nods slowly. "Okay. I guess that makes sense."

"You guess? You made me feel like shit the moment you saw me at the front door."

"That wasn't because of *you*. Not really."

"What the hell does that mean?"

Keifer sucks his lower lip into his mouth and shakes his head. 'It's complicated."

I close my eyes in frustration. "Listen, I know it's a lot to take in and you didn't ask for me to keep it, so I really don't expect you to care or do anything. Okay? You're off the hook."

"Is that what you want?"

I sigh. "I don't know, Keifer. This is a lot all at once. I don't know how to process that you know when I was trying so hard to keep it a secret from you."

His hand moves the rest of the way to me now. "May I?"

I warily lift my hand and put it in his. It feels good to have a bit of tenderness after all of our depravity.

"I admit that when I found out, I was totally out of sorts. But I've thought about it, and I know now that I want to be a part of the baby's life. As much as you'll allow me to be."

I have to pick my jaw up off the floor I'm so shocked. I didn't think a young, sexy guy like Keifer would want anything to do with an accidental pregnancy. "Seriously?"

He nods. "I've always known I've wanted kids. I thought it would be more on my terms, but..." He half-laughs. "That's kind of the nature of these things, isn't it? Happens when you least expect it."

"Tell me about it. It's totally thrown a wrench in my plans."

"I'm sorry, I guess."

We both laugh. "Takes two to tango."

"And we tangoed pretty hard."

"Trust me, I remember."

Our eyes meet briefly before we both look away shyly, as if we haven't seen each other naked and fucked five ways to Sunday.

For once, it feels like we're connected. The three of us. One hand on my belly, the other in Keifer's. Not a conventional family, but a start of something like it.

What that something is...who the hell knows.

But for once, I don't feel so alone.

I hope Dara can't see me staring at the hand cupping her belly, but I can't help it. I didn't realize how *real* it was. Her sweatshirts and T-shirts have been hiding it so well, but now that it's obvious...it's really *obvious*. There's a noticeable curve to her stomach, so apparent on her small and lithe frame.

That's my baby. Our baby.

"I appreciate you wanting to be a part of this. Even if you've been a jerk to me the past few months."

I hide my face in my hand and Dara laughs. "Trust me, I feel like an absolute jerk now. If I had known you were pregnant, I wouldn't have put you through all that."

"You're right, I have been in near constant duress," Dara says with a smirk, eyes rolling to the side.

"I know you're joking, but seriously. I made you pass out. You could have been hurt. Or...well, I don't want to think about what could have happened."

She nods. "Yeah. Me either."

We're both quiet for a moment.

"Still, though, I'm kinda glad you were being a pain in

the ass." Dara removes her hand from mine. "Made for a lot of fun arguments."

"Arguments? Is that what you'd call them?"

She grins. "What would *you* call them?"

"Uhhh...no, arguments is a good way to put it."

Dara laughs, her big free laugh. I'm not sure if I've heard it quite like that since the night we met. She's probably been through so much trying to navigate being pregnant unexpectedly.

I know I couldn't have known. But I feel like I should have. Like some innate piece of me should have sensed that out there a woman was carrying my baby. The fact I didn't know and put her through hell, regardless of how innocent my pranks may have been breaks my heart.

Makes me feel unworthy.

I have to make up for it any way that I can. "I know I'm not your favorite guy, probably. And you don't owe me anything. I totally get it if you want me to fuck off. But I really hope you don't. You know?"

Dara laughs smally. "I promise. I don't want you to fuck off. Although we probably need to get the swearing thing in check before the baby's born."

I nod. "I've already been practicing that since we have so many babies in the family now."

Dara looks into her lap. Something's on her mind. Something she might not know how to say. I know that feeling.

"I'm really grateful that you're not running away from this. I know it's a lot. And I kind of made this decision for the both of us. Or... I guess I made it for me. So I'm glad you're willing to be okay with that decision."

"Yeah. More than okay with it."

"Good. Good..."

We sink into silence again. We're used to that. Lots of silences full of lust and rage and now… Tenderness?

"You must think I'm crazy for being so young and unestablished and wanting a baby." Her eyes are downcast.

"No. Not at all. I already feel called to caring for our child and I'm not even the one carrying it. I can't imagine what that must feel like."

Dara looks to me, rims of her eyes reddening. "It's scary but feels right. Right?"

"Yeah. Totally."

She touches one of the flowers, stroking the velvet petals between her fingers. "You know, I don't have any family. And going about this alone is terrifying. But then I kept thinking that at the end of it all, I wouldn't be alone. You know, I'd have a baby. And a bakery. Hopefully."

I laugh. She's able to make even the saddest sentences glimmer with hope. "What happened? To your family. If you don't mind me asking."

Dara's hazel eyes, wet with tears unshed, look at me with alarm.

"You don't have to tell me."

"I can. It's just…a lot, so forgive me if I –" She gestures to her face. "I'm already more emotional than I would be in normal circumstances."

"You don't have to apologize, Dara. I'm here. I'm listening."

Dara takes a deep breath. "Well. We were all really close. I was the only child. And my dreams were their dreams. And vice versa. My mom is who taught me to bake. She was the heart of the operation. Was going to be. You see, ever since I was little, I wanted to be a baker. There was never another option. Desserts and how they made people light up at the end of a meal, that was everything to me. No matter who you are, you like dessert. Even if you say you don't like sweets. There's something. Cake, cookies, fruit salad–"

"Fruit salad?"

"Oh, there's an art to fruit salad, Keifer. You've never had my mom's." A smile creeps over her lips. She gets up and goes to a shelf of books built into one of the cabinets, retrieving what looks to be a handbound manuscript. Dara puts it on the table and sits back down. "She had a recipe for every sweet treat you could think of." She turns through the pages quickly, turns the book around, and slides it toward me. "Even fruit salad."

Sure enough, I'm looking at a recipe for fruit salad. The page is photocopied from a handwritten document. And on it is a little drawing of a bowl with fruit in it. Clearly done by a child. "Is this your handiwork?" I ask, pointing to the drawing.

Dara grins. "You got it."

"You were a dynamic duo, huh?"

She nods. "Trio, really. Mom with heart, me with skills, and dad with the checkbook."

I chuckled. "Sounds familiar."

"When I got old enough, I decided I wanted to go to Madison and start my own bakery. So we found a perfect little building right by the lake. Downstairs we'd run bakery, upstairs we'd live. A real family business. And it was all going to plan." Dara's smile breaks. Darkness crosses her face. "And then three weeks before they were supposed to come and join me in Madison...there was a gas leak back at their house." She stays quiet for a couple of seconds. I stay quiet too because I know this is not a happy story.

Her whispered words rip into me like knives. "They

never even noticed. Just fell asleep… never to wake up again."

My heart falls. I didn't expect her story to be just so tragic. Not beautiful, bubbly Dara. "Jesus Christ, Dara. I'm so sorry."

"Three weeks. That was it. You know? It always happens like that. Sad things. The universe loves just snatching things from you at the last moment." She starts playing with the hem of her sweatshirt. "So, I had to use all the money for funeral expenses and pay off the debt for the shop and the building because unless someone miraculously bought it, I was stuck with it. I've been falling further and further behind over the years and am just about to catch up."

"Did they have life insurance?"

Dara nods. "For some reason, the insurance company keeps giving me the runaround. Implying potentially foul play. But there's no credible evidence. So they just keep investigating and investigating and opening up this wound I'm trying to close. But I guess the fucked-up part is that…" She lets out a breath, giving into the weight on her shoulders. Tears start to stream down her cheeks. "It'll never be closed. It'll always be open. And here I am, alone and maimed and trying to survive and make them proud and…it hurts so much." She covers her face with her hands. Embarrassed.

I know that pain. The loss that feels unfair. My mother. Taken from us, driving to pick up my dad from a work thing when he was too drunk to drive home himself. A freak accident. Unfair. A moment in time. Could happen to anyone.

Feels like a curse.

I know in this moment it's not helpful for me to recount all of my pain to Dara. I touch her elbow. The tension in her body softens, but she does not reveal her face. I pull her into me. Regardless of who we are to each other, what frustration we've caused one another, how our bodies have been intertwined, Dara needs my comfort.

She weeps into my shoulder. I hold her close, let her cry it out. From time to time my mind drifts to her lower half that is still tilted away from me. I don't know if she'll ever let me feel, but I hope upon hope she finds it in her heart to let me.

Dara draws away from me. My arms feel empty. "Sorry. I knew I'd cry, but not this much." Dara smiles through the last wave of tears.

"It's okay. You gotta let it out. Thank you for telling me."

Her lips and nose have reddened from crying. It honestly makes her look so cute. I want to take care of her.

Slow down, Keif. You've got quite a few hoops to jump through before that. "I promise, Dara. You're not alone. I'm here. As much as you need. As far as the baby is concerned. And you. You know, I think we at least ought to be friends if we're having a baby together."

She laughs. "Yes, that's the least we could do probably."

I close the recipe book and put one hand on it and one in the air. "I, Keifer Hawthorn, promise you, Dara Palmer, that I will always be here for our unborn child. Through thick and thin, right or wrong, day or night...whatever."

She grins.

"I'm here."

I slide the book across to her. "Your turn."

"I, Dara Palmer, promise you, Keifer Hawthorn..."

I can barely hear what she's saying through my thoughts spiraling out of control, imagining what this would feel like if we were standing in front of an officiant. Sure, the words are different, but it's still a promise from the depths of our souls.

Could I handle that? Marrying Dara? Not that she'd say yes if I asked.

I guess I'll have to see.

"...thick and thin...right or wrong...day or night. I'm here."

"Cool."

Cool??? This woman is having your baby and all you can manage is "cool"?? Get it together. "Living next door to one another is already a pretty good start, huh?"

"Sure is. As long as I'm allowed to stay here."

I roll my eyes. "Okay, we are long past the stage of me trying to get you to move out."

"Oh yeah? When did that change?"

"Gosh...I don't know. Probably when you got so mad at me and then we...in the kitchen?"

"Oh my god. Yeah. Guess that did change a lot."

"But I promise, I'll never ask you to leave again. In fact, I think it'd probably make the most sense if we're going to be trying to raise this baby together if we both stayed. As long as we can. You know?"

Dara nods eagerly. "Totally. But I don't want to hold you back. You know, I'm gonna be in Chicago hopefully forever. I don't know where you're going to be off to with all your big business plans."

"Ah, trust me. I don't want to go far. But if things change, we need each other's consent. Does that seem fair? For the baby."

"Yeah. For the baby." Dara looks away and chews on her lower lip. "You want to feel?"

Every nerve in my body is alight. "Y-yes. If that's okay. Is that weird?"

"No. I offered."

"I know, but only if you're okay with it."

"Keifer. Here." She takes my hand and puts against her stomach.

I hold my breath as I take in the way the curve of her stomach fits into the palm of my hand.

"It's not moving yet. But soon, hopefully."

"Yeah...yeah, wow. This is incredible."

Her hand splays out against mine. I've never felt closer to a person. How could I? She's chosen to carry my baby. I'm inextricably linked to her. Inside her.

I'm terrified.

And despite the innocence of the moment and the grand love that we are sharing for this unborn baby, I remember how I felt the other night, imagining being with her again. I try to push the thought from my mind, but it keeps returning, especially now that I know how it feels.

"Dara, listen...I know we got off on the wrong foot."

"Which time? The one-night-stand or the pranking me until I break?"

"You're not gonna let me live that down, are you?"

She laughs, relaxing into her chair. "Never."

"Well, okay. I think we deserve a second – no, *third* chance at getting to know one another. How does that sound?"

"Good. Yeah...really good."

I twist my lips to the side. "I'm not sure where it could lead. You know, I don't want to make any promises or make you feel like you owe me more than just this. But I'd at the very least like to be friends."

"Me too." Dara takes my hand away from her stomach and turns it into a handshake. "Hi. I'm Dara Palmer."

I laugh and shake her hand. "Keifer Hawthorn. Nice to meet you."

"I heard I'm having your baby."

I sharply inhale. She has no idea what that sentence does to my body and soul. "I believe you're correct."

The ride home from work is grueling, not to mention it's an unusually hot day for the beginning of June. At four and a half months, I shouldn't feel as big as I am, but it's becoming more and more obvious. Now, I'm opting for loose dresses rather than sweaters and sweatpants. Sometimes the fabric swings just so that I'm afraid someone is going to point and scream out that I'm pregnant.

Just being paranoid, though.

It takes me nearly an hour more than usual to get home after every mode of public transportation seems to fail inexplicably. By the time I get home, it's dusk and I'm exhausted.

As I walk onto the cul-de-sac, I find myself smiling for the first time.

Now that Keifer knows, I don't need to hide anymore. Even more than that, he's willing to be a part of the baby's life. That means we can share more than just practical jokes and bouts of angry fucking.

We have a future together. What it looks like, neither of

us knows. But I don't care. My baby is going to have a father. That makes me want to jump for joy.

Just as I'm thinking of Keifer, he comes out onto his front stoop and waves. "Hey. You're home late."

"Yeah. The train broke down like three times and then we got stuck on Lawrence behind a huge fender bender. It was...well, it's not interesting. I'm exhausted. And starving. I ate a whole thing of tic-tac's on the way home."

"Nutritious!" he says, waggling his eyebrows.

"It's all I had. Better than nothing." I got to my front door and start to unlock it, the little blue apple catching my eye. I smile to myself.

"So, it sounds like you need some dinner."

I glance at Keifer. "Oh, yeah. I've got some leftovers from yesterday I was about to heat up."

He frowns. "After all of that trouble? No. You need a fresh, homecooked meal."

"Do you have a suggestion?"

He beams. "I'll be over in a minute."

Keifer disappears into the house. I'm stunned. Is he... coming over to cook me dinner?

Sure enough, just a minute or two later, Keifer waltzes into my house with bags of groceries. Did he plan this?

He drops the bags on the counter with a thud and then rifles through them. "Alright, first things first. Chicken or fish?"

I stare at him. "Uh..."

"It's not a hard question, Dara."

"Sorry, I'm just confused?"

"Does it help if I say the fish is halibut?"

I smile in bewilderment. "Uh. Chicken, I guess."

"Okay. Chicken. Now broccoli or brussel sprouts?"

"Ugh. Veggies?!"

"You're pregnant, Dara. You need the iron and the fiber. You can't just eat cookies and cupcakes all the time."

"Hey!" I jab him in the side with my finger. "It's part of my job!"

Keifer eyes me. "Yes, and now it's part of my job to make sure you're taking good care of yourself. Because regardless of what caused you to faint the other day, I am not taking any chances. So, A or B?"

I grunt. "Broccoli. Just no onions. They make me nauseous."

Keifer's eyebrows jump. He whips off his phone and types something into his notes. "Here. Make a list for me of all the stuff that makes you sick so I can avoid it, alright?"

I take his phone. "You're so funny."

"No, I'm thorough. Pasta or rice?"

"Pasta. That one is easy."

"Perfect. Now you sit. Enjoy a–" He pulls a sparkling water out of his bag. "A seltzer. And relax. You had a long day."

I shake my head. "I can help."

"Uh-uh. You're not going to lift a finger."

"Keifer, I'm like barely pregnant. So I'd prefer you save this energy for further down the line when I'm having to waddle from place to place. I can help."

He looks at me incredulously. "Dara, this isn't like a coupon you use up. I'm trying to take care of you. The baby. Let me do that, huh?"

Keifer says it so resolutely that I don't feel I have a choice but to take a seat at the kitchen table, prop my feet up, and let him go to town.

I have to say, it feels pretty nice being waited on like this. And I didn't expect that this was the kind of help and support he would be giving.

As Keifer cooks in a way that would make any chef cringe, pots and pans everywhere and scraps falling to the floor, we talk. He tells me about his day, I tell him about mine. He asks for updates about my bakery. He's...friendly. Like the man that I met that first night. Adam. Except this time there's no lasciviousness, no end game to his kindness.

It's just Keifer. And I like it.

Once dinner is all cooked up and miraculously the kitchen is clean, Keifer sets a plate out in front of me. "Chicken piccata, broccoli, angel hair pasta. No onions. Bon appetit."

My eyes grow as wide as the plate in front of me. "Wow, this looks amazing."

Keifer sits across from me with a smug smile. "Why don't you taste it and see if it lives up to expectations?"

I take one bite. Every flavor melts on my tongue. I would swear the baby flipped in my belly if I didn't know better. "Mmm. Delicious."

I eat ravenously. The stress of the day melts as my belly fills.

"Better than tic-tac's or leftovers, right?"

"Much better," I say through a mouthful of pasta.

"Okay, easy," he chuckles. He's a much more polite eater than I am, but I can't help it. I'm eating for two after all.

I have seconds, even of the broccoli, to Keifer's delight. I am sated beyond compare, leaning back in my chair and stretching out. "That was...wow."

"Good, huh?"

"Great. Where'd you learn to cook like that?"

"Well, I was mom's helper during dinner. That's what happens when you're the youngest."

I smile softly. I know Keifer lost his mother when he

was young as well. Maybe he'll tell me that story some time. I'd love to hear it.

"Now, you can say no, but..." he says, eyeing the grocery bags that are still plentiful on the counter.

"But..."

"I thought if you were up for it, you could make me some of that famous fruit salad. I'll be your helper."

I grin. I haven't made my mom's fruit salad in ages. After all, who really wants fruit salad when you want a sweet treat? But, to Keifer's point, I'm pregnant and a baker. Perhaps I should take it easy on the really sweet treats. "What kind of fruit did you get?" I get to my feet and go to open the bag.

"Um. Well. Don't be mad. But I do have a spare key."

"Yeah, I got that after all my sugar turned into salt," I say, glaring back at him.

Keifer flushes. It's so cute when he's embarrassed. He's usually so smooth that it breaks his charismatic demeanor. "I checked the recipe before I went to the store. I can give you the key back if it makes you uncomfortable."

I start to remove all the fruit from the bag: grapes, blueberries, kiwi, the list goes on. "No, keep it. You might need it when I call you in the middle of the night with a craving and I can't get out of bed to answer the door."

He chuckles. "I'll be there. Promise."

My heart flutters. His promise is for our baby. Not for me. But I can't help but swoon...a man waiting on me hand and foot while I do the intense biological work of growing his child. There's something so innately romantic about it.

"Okay. Come here, Chef Keifer. And listen closely."

After explaining to Keifer how exactly I want all the fruit cut up, I start to work on the syrup. That's the trick. Fruit salad is never just fruit sitting in a bowl. There's a lot of work that goes into it. And my mom perfected the recipe. Lemon juice, orange juice, brown sugar, vanilla extract. *Perfection*. Once it's mixed to perfection, throw it in the freezer to cool fast.

Keifer is cutting the fruit exactly to my specifications, but he's going at about half the speed I would.

"I didn't know you were part sloth," I tease as I sneak in beside him.

"I'm trying to get it right! Slow and steady wins the race, Dara."

Instead of intervening like I'd planned, I watch his methodical cuts. *Slow and steady wins the race.* Everything's been moving so fast the past few months. I've gotten swept up in always having to go, go, go.

Here with Keifer, I can take a breath. I never could have anticipated that him knowing about the baby would be the thing that frees me.

Keifer scrapes his spoon around the inside of his bowl. "Okay. You're right. That is *amazing* fruit salad."

"Lick the bowl, why don't you?"

"It's good! What do you want from me?"

I settle back into my place on the couch with a sigh, resting my hands on my stomach. "I'm just giving you a hard time."

His green eyes sparkle. "Yeah, I can tell."

I need to stay grounded. Just because we're having a baby doesn't mean that anything is going to happen between us. But sometimes, the little turn of his eye or the way he smiles makes me melt. I have no reason to believe that we have what it takes for anything romantic. There's chemistry, sure, but that isn't all that you need for a relationship.

We'd need an emotional connection. Trust. Commitment.

Those aren't things you can just turn on.

"Here. Let me take these." Keifer collects the dishes.

"I'd help you if my body wasn't fused to the couch already."

He laughs. "No, you rest. You need it."

Whatever woman ends up with him will be very lucky. When he's not being an asshole, he's incredibly sweet and attentive. And the thought of him with another woman does something inside my chest that makes me really uncomfortable. I shift in my seat.

"Ah!" I sit up suddenly, a sharp pain running through my lower back.

I hear the bowls clatter in the sink. Keifer rushes back into the room. "What is it, what's wrong?!"

I rub my lower back. "Oh, sorry. I didn't mean to scare you. I've just been getting cramps in my lower back since, you know, the whole pregnancy thing."

"Can I get you anything to help?"

"No, it should pass. And if it doesn't, I'll just get out my heating pad."

Keifer stares at me, wringing his hands.

"Keifer. This is normal."

"I know, but after seeing you faint, I'm jumpy."

I sigh. "Well, get used to it. Pregnancy is just all weird shit like this."

"Do you want some help?"

I look at him with alarm. What does he mean by help? Why is my mind so far in the gutter that I immediately think he means that sex will be the thing to help? Because admittedly, it would, especially with how my hormones have been raging.

"I could give you a massage if you were comfortable with it."

I sigh in relief. "Oh. Uh. Yeah. Sure. You don't have to, though."

"It's the least I can do."

Everything Keifer has offered this evening has been "the least he could do". By the time my pregnancy is completed, I'm going to owe him so many favors.

Keifer doesn't wait for me to respond. He sits beside me on the couch and holds up his hands. "May I?"

"Y-yeah..." I turn around so my back is facing him.

As soon as his hands are on me, my body relaxes. It's like my nerves were hungering for his touch. But I'm not about to stop him now. I'll ride it out.

His hands knead my lower back firmly, but carefully. "How's that feel?"

Fucking amazing. "Good."

"You can direct me if you want."

"Um. Okay. A little to the right."

His hands move, hitting right upon the cramping area.

"Oh, fuck. Yeah. That's it."

Keifer laughs. I feel his breath on my ear. I'd love to lean back into him and kiss him. *That's not what this is, Dara. Settle down.*

As his fingers work my back through my shirt, the fabric starts to inch up the slightest bit. I feel his thumb graze my skin and then jerk away as if I've burnt him.

"Sorry."

Don't be sorry.

Keifer pulls my shirt down definitively. I resist sighing sadly.

"That's great. Thank you." I move away from his touch. Any more than that and I might do something stupid.

We smile at one another shyly.

"I'm feeling kind of tired."

Keifer nods vehemently. "Yeah. Of course. You need your rest." He gets to his feet and starts for the door. "I'll get out of your hair."

I'd want nothing more than for him to be *in* my hair. "Thank you so much for everything."

"Yeah. Any time."

As soon as he's out of the house, it's quiet. So unbearably quiet that I feel his absence all the way from my head to my toes.

Alone again. Perhaps not mentally and emotionally, but still, physically.

That's when I swear that in my belly, I feel a flutter. A quickening. Brief and so small I'm almost not sure if it was real. My hand flies to my stomach. "Was that you?" My eyes fill with tears.

Not physically alone. Never again.

"You sure you don't want to wait until you know the gender?"

Dara looks around the room. I've always hated this one because the walls are so dark. Navy blue but worse somehow. The only saving grace is the big window that looks out onto my house. "Do we really need to be all gendered about the color of the baby's nursery, Keifer?"

"Well, no, but –"

"Listen, I have time today to pick out a color for the nursery. It's in my schedule," she says adamantly.

I've become familiar with Dara's *schedule*. Her life is planned out to a T. I thought *I* was a workaholic. I'm a slacker when it comes to her. There's barely a moment she doesn't have planned out between work, planning her business, and lightly preparing for the baby's arrival. In fact, she's been so busy she missed her last appointment with her OB, during which she could have learned the gender of the baby. I gave her a lot of shit for that, but that was before I even knew about the existence of the baby so I can't be *too* critical.

Today, one of the few Saturdays she has off, she's enlisted me to help her pick out a paint color for the nursery. At first, she'd wanted me to help her paint the whole thing, but I'd insisted on hiring painters for the job. Dara was resistant because of the cost. She hasn't quite caught onto my nearly bottomless checkbook yet.

On one of the navy walls, there is a coating of white primer that's just dried. We have about eight different mini cans of test paint. Dara was trigger happy at Ace Hardware picking out shades. The joke being almost all of them are varieties of cream and beige. Whatever. It's her house.

"Alright. Let's get started, then, huh? Which shade first?" I hold up a can. "How about Big Bend Beige?"

"Sounds perfect."

I crack open the can and give it a mix with a paint stick. "Look at that exciting, droopy skin color..."

"Keifer!"

"I'm sorry, but come on! This is a *sad* color."

Dara takes a paint brush and dips it in the paint. "A nursery isn't *just* paint, jackass. It's going to be the furniture and decorations and it'll be much more exciting than Big Bend Beige, okay?" She slathers the paint on the wall.

We both stare at it. Literally watching paint dry.

"Okay. You're right. It's ugly," she concedes.

"Ha! See ya, Big Bend Beige!"

"Ugh, you're impossible."

I have to act a little foolish to keep things casual between us. If I'm not always joking, that leaves room for silence. Leaves room for questions. And *for now* there's no time or room for that. All of our focus is on the baby and keeping things platonic so that we can form a relationship beyond the physical.

That doesn't mean I'm not thinking about her in *that*

way, though. Dara's started wearing clothing that shows off her growing stomach better, and sometimes I catch myself staring. She's just *so* beautiful and her beauty is heightened by knowing she's carrying my baby.

So I've got to keep myself from falling in too deep.

Dara picks up another can, lips twisted in annoyance. "It sounds like if you had your way, you'd paint the whole room that ugly blue color you chose for my front stoop."

I laugh. "No, even *I* wouldn't be able to stand that after a while. Besides, that'd definitely be for a boy, wouldn't it?"

She smirks at me and tosses the next paint can my way. I catch it easily. "Silver Lake. You can do the honors."

Again, pop open the can, stir it with the stick. This time, I take a brush and paint a streak onto the wall. "Mm. Gray. Thrilling."

"Listen! You can't be so negative, Keifer!"

"I'm not being negative! We've got a bunch of options. I'm holding out for a hero, alright?"

Dara laughs. "You're impossible."

"Whatever. Silver Lake's out." I start to move the can to join Big Bend Beige on the floor, but Dara grabs the paint can, trying to tug it out of my hand.

"My house, my paint. Silver Lake is a yes for me."

Her eyes are determined, boring into mine. "You're the boss."

"You're damn right."

We try out a couple more colors. A yellower beige, which we both like, a gray that skews rather blue that is a maybe, and a color that even Dara can't justify as being any different than white.

"So, do you have a guess?" I ask, moving onto the next can.

"What do you mean?"

"About the gender. Don't expectant mothers sometimes get a feeling?"

Dara frowns and touches her stomach thoughtlessly. I love when she does that. It's become a default for her when she's thinking about the baby. It makes her even more adorable. "Um, I don't know. I mean, educated guess, you only have brothers. So maybe a boy?"

"No, not an educated guess, Palmer."

She giggles at my old nickname for her.

"A *feeling*. A gut instinct."

Dara sighs. "I don't have time for gut feelings. I deal with facts and figures, you know? Recipes require precision. Not guessing."

"I've never taken you for a facts and figures girl."

"Why? Because I'm blonde."

"Uh. Yeah."

Dara sticks her fingers into the paint can I've just opened and flicks droplets of paint onto my shirt.

"Hey!"

"Your fault for calling me a dumb blonde."

"I didn't call you a *dumb* blonde! It was a joke!"

She sniffles phonily. "I'm sensitive, Keifer!"

"Oh, you're so full of shit." I dip my fingers into the paint and flick some her way too.

She squeals. "You're so asking for it!"

You bet your ass I'm asking for it.

Dara pulls the paint stick out of the can and smacks it against my thigh.

"I recall this isn't the *first* time you've covered me in paint."

"It's not my fault you're always being an asshole," she snickers.

I shrug. "Guess you're right." I take the mostly full paint

can and fake her out by acting like I'm going to cover in her paint. She throws up her hands defensively and I chuckle. "Don't worry, I'd never." Instead, I splash it toward the wall. It lands in a thick coating, dripping down the wall.

"Oh my god! You're making a mess!" she's trying her best to be admonishing, but the smile on her face says everything. She's having fun.

We're having fun.

"Actually..." She trails off and puts her hands on her hips. "I think I like it."

I look past the mess, actually seeing the color for the first time. It's a light yellow. Subtle. Not like the stereotypical baby nursery yellow that reminds me of a sickening hospital room curtain. This one is nice. "Me too."

Dara smiles at me. "Glad we can agree."

"Now let's get out of here before the fumes go to your head."

She nods eagerly. "Good idea."

We close the door and rush around the house to open windows to let the paint dry. Then, we head outside, sitting on the backsteps leading down to the backyard.

"I honestly never thought we were going to agree," Dara says, leaning her head on her hand.

"Yeah. Me either. Because you're so opinionated."

Dara punches me playfully on the arm. "The nursery's in *my* house, Keifer."

"Yeah. I know. I'm just teasing..." The nursery *is* in her house. The baby will be staying with her. As it should be. She's the mother after all. But I can't help but feel a little sad that the baby won't be sleeping at my house. Sure, I'm not looking forward to being woken up by crying, but I've always dreamed of being able to go into my baby's nursery in the morning to wake him or her up. Watching them stretch out and, eventually, smile because they're happy to see me.

Wow, I'm much softer than I realized.

"Do you think maybe the baby should have a room at my house too? Like a nursery?"

Dara frowns. "You think we should split nights?"

I shrug. "I don't know. I just would feel weird staying right next door and making you do all the work when I could be helping. You know?"

She looks down at the toes of her dirty snickers. "I don't know, Keifer. You have an important job. You need your rest."

"Well, so do you. I mean, opening a bakery is going to be a lot of work. Between doing that during the day and taking care of a baby at night, that's going to be a lot. Especially if you're shouldering it alone."

Dara bites her lower lip, thinking.

"Like I said when we first started this. The amount I'm in the baby's life is entirely at your discretion, but I'd really like to –"

"As long as it's not that ugly blue color, fine. I think that could work."

We exchange a smile. "Thanks."

"No, thank you. I can't imagine many guys in your situation would be eager for sleepless nights. You're either special or a crazy person."

"I like to think I'm a well-balanced mix of both." I wink playfully at her.

Dara nods. "Sounds about right."

Having a nursery in my house is a big step. It really means that we are going to be splitting the work of taking care of the baby. I should be terrified to be saddled with the responsibility. And while I am, I'm also excited. For the change. I've been moving on autopilot for a few years now. Traveling, working, fucking around.

This is going to change everything.

"And we should take down the fence. Don't you think?"

"Yeah, and make a bridge connecting the top floors."

"Totally."

Dara eyes me. "I was kidding, Keifer."

I flush. "Oh. Yeah. Me too."

"Sky's the limit with you, isn't it?"

"What do you mean?"

Dara looks off across the yard. It needs some TLC, that's for sure. Landscaping, and we'll definitely need to put in a jungle gym, swing set, and a sandbox. I'm getting ahead of myself. But I can't help it. I've already created memories to be for my baby. And it's not even here yet.

"You have the money to kind of do whatever you want. A baby's just a drop in the bucket for you. You're going to be able to give our baby a life I would have had to grind for years for." She swallows. "I feel sort of inadequate."

"Are you kidding, Dara? You're perfectly adequate. More than. Obviously."

"Is it obvious?"

If we were closer, I'd reach out and touch her. Hold her hands, grab her knee, wrap her up in my arms and make sure she hears this loud and clear. I grip my fists tightly to keep myself from touching her. "You're carrying a baby. You were prepared to do everything you could to care for it on your own. Sure, it would have been really hard. But you were going to do it. That decision alone means a lot more than money, I think."

She smiles, the apples of her cheeks bold and full. "That means a lot."

"I mean every word."

Dara leans her head on my shoulder. My breath freezes. *Stay calm, Keifer. Don't get hard. Don't do anything stupid. She's just the mother of your child.* And god help me if that last thought doesn't make everything that much more over-whelming.

"It's going to be good," she murmurs.

I cautiously wrap my arm around her. That's alright, right? "Not just good, Dara. It's going to be *great*."

Her face is filled with contentment. Maybe something more. I try not to read into it. I point to some dried paint in a strand of her hair. "You got something right there."

She flushes. "Oh. Wonder what that could be?"

I laugh. "Here." I gently scrape the paint off her hair until it's clean and blonde again.

"You too." She reaches up and removes a chunk of paint from my bangs.

I swallow and glance down at her belly and then back into her hazel eyes. Those eyes are becoming more and more like home every day. "We're a little family right here."

Dara giggles. "Yeah?"

"Yeah."

"Is that what you'd call us? Even though you didn't even know my name when we conceived this baby and we've been the best of enemies for months now?"

I don't care how we met or what happened after. Now that I know, my heart knows. "Yeah. It is what I would call us."

Surprise spreads across Dara's face. "I like the sound of that."

I'd love to kiss her. But I'll be good. I'll resist. For now.

I've avoided stepping into a store for babies as long as I could have. However, having already past the twenty-weeks mark a couple of weeks back, it's time to get serious.

"Dara, you're going to need a car."

We've been walking down the car seat aisle, which has taken an obscene amount of time. Keifer is reading the specs on *every single* one as if he was buying an entire car, not just the car seat.

"I don't have money for a car," I say.

"I'll buy it for you, of course."

"Keifer, seriously. No."

"How are you going to get the baby places?"

I snort. "In a stroller? On public transportation? Like lots of people?"

Keifer shakes his head. "I don't like that."

I lean on one of the shelves. "What do you mean, you don't *like that*?"

"I don't want you traveling around the city on public transportation with the baby in a stroller. It doesn't sound safe. I'd rather you be in a car."

I frown. "Keifer, you're not my *keeper,* you know?"

"That's not what this is about." He squats down to look at one of the car seats. "This is about you two being safe."

While I am a little annoyed that Keifer is making decisions about what I can and can't do with the baby, it does make me happy he cares so much. "I can't accept a whole *car.*"

He looks up at me. His hair is messier than usual. A casual day off of work for him. Just a T-shirt, jeans, and a mop of blond hair. While he looks incredible in his work clothes, this is a whole different side of him. Casual Keifer does something to me. It makes me feral. I want to kiss him sloppily and drag him into a broom closet so we can do nasty things.

I push my fingernail into my palm. This is my new technique for whenever I get too turned on by Keifer. If I associate my horniness with pain, it'll go away eventually, right? *Right?!*

"When's your birthday?" Keifer asks.

"December."

"Dammit. What day?"

"The twenty-second?"

"Of course you're a Christmastime baby."

"What's that mean?"

"It means that you were born during the most wonderful time of year. You give off that energy."

I try not to be too flattered by that.

"Because you're so bubbly and sweet." Keifer looks down at his smart watch and taps around on it. "Okay. It'll be a half-birthday present."

"What will be?"

"Your car, Dara. We'll add it to the list of things we have to do."

I try to refuse, but Keifer cuts me off. "You can't refuse a half-birthday present. That'd be rude, don't you think?"

I gape at him. "You're impossible."

Keifer ignores me and goes back down the aisle to a car seat model we looked at earlier. "We'll get two of these."

I resist looking at the price tag. Keifer's taste is obviously very high-end. Money is never an object. It still puts a lump in my stomach when I'm always having to think about where to allocate my money between my bills, debts, and dreams.

"Okay, strollers next?"

We wind through the store to the stroller section with a cart that has filled up with various odds and ends that have caught our eye through the store. We certainly have baby fever in that things that are little and cute are things we *must-have* regardless of how practical. We don't even know if we are having a boy or a girl and we already have onesies for both.

Sure, we also have a lot of the must-haves too. And, as much as spending all this money is freaking me out, I'm having fun. Keifer and I have built a rapport the past week and a half between activities for the baby and dinners that have become almost nightly.

There's nothing like sharing a fetus to make you fast friends.

My phone rings in my purse and I pull it out. *Rye Linden.*

"Who's that?"

"Spam." I let it go to voicemail.

Spending so much time with Keifer has taken my time away from other things. For one, the plans for the bakery are falling a bit to the wayside. And Rye...

Rye's on my ass all the time. Texting, calling. I don't

know how she has so much time to hound me. She even showed up to the house unannounced one evening, furious that I was ignoring her. Thank god Keifer wasn't over or else I would have probably blabbed the whole truth without being prompted.

I'm not trying to ignore her. But I'm not ready to be honest with her that Keifer's the father of my baby.

Keifer and I have discussed the family's reaction. And both of us are unsure of how to go about it. For one, Keifer is now adding to a family lineage of accidental pregnancies, almost as if they've been cursed (or blessed?) by a witch. As for me, I barely know his family. I don't know how I'd fit in and don't know if I'd have the energy to start at this point in time.

"Oh, Dara. Look at this!"

Keifer stops in front of a display of the softest looking stuffed animals. He points to a white duck stuffy that sits up on its bottom, looking strange and adorable.

"It's a duck."

"I know. It's so cute. I need it. For the baby of course."

I laugh. "Of course. Although, no one is ever too old for stuffed animals, Keifer."

He picks up the duck lovingly. "What's that mean?"

"I'm just saying..." I poke him in the ribs. "You can buy the stuffed animal for *you* if you love it so much."

He flushes red as a beet. "For me! No! No way."

"Are you sure? Because you're clutching it to your chest like you love it."

Keifer looks down at the stuffy in his arms and then throws it in the cart haphazardly. "Shut up."

I laugh. "Awww! You love the duck, don't you?"

"Listen, you –" Keifer reaches out and tickles my sides.

"Stop! You know I'm ticklish!" I push him off. We're both laughing loudly.

Yeah. Just friends. Who tickle and tease each other in public and are having a baby together. Super chill.

"Well, you two are just adorable!"

We turn to find an older woman wearing a nametag and red vest, clearly an employee at the store. She's grinning at us.

I glance at Keifer. "Oh...thank you..." I say nervously. There's no reason to break her heart and tell her we're not together. But still, it's a little awkward.

"When are you due?" she asks, coming closer to us.

"October fourteenth," I say. Though it's only June, saying that out loud makes it sound so close.

"Oh, you've still got a bit then. Good on you for getting started on shopping early. It's going to go faster than you know it."

"Yeah. Already feel that," Keifer says wryly. After all, he's only known about the baby a few weeks. I resist thwapping him in the ribs.

The older woman looks between us. "Well, it's good to see two parents getting involved. It's my favorite part of the job, seeing young parents so hopeful. It's your first, right?"

"Yeah. Can you tell?" Keifer grins.

"Oh, absolutely! First-timers give off an energy. They're nervous, excited, still totally in love."

Totally in love, huh? She's either making shit up or reading something I'm trying to avoid.

I feel Keifer shift toward me, his hip brushing up against my side. "Maybe you can walk us through the strollers? We're still new at this, as you can tell."

"I'd love to! Follow me!"

We follow the woman, whose name we learn is Rita,

over to the strollers. She starts spewing all the details about every make and model. Thank god Keifer is listening, because her explanations are landing on my deaf ears. All I can think about is how *cute* she thought we were together and how we look like we're in love.

I don't know if I *love* Keifer. I know we have chemistry. I know I love our baby. But do I love Keifer?

I know I could.

I know I most likely do already.

I watch him asking questions, testing out different strollers, making jokes. From time to time, he turns to me to ask for my opinion or how I'm feeling.

"You're so attentive!" Rita says, squeezing Keifer's arm. "I wish all fathers-to-be were like that."

"Well, it's the least I can do. She's doing all the real work," he says, running his hand down my back gently.

I feel like crying. This onslaught of confusing emotions is too much. We aren't together, but now he's acting like we are, and Rita *thinks* we are. Now I'm *wishing* we were.

It's a lot to take in.

"Dara? Dara, did you hear me?"

I snap out of my trance. "Huh? What?"

"What do you think of this guy?" Keifer pushes a stroller forward. It looks more like a tactical vehicle than a stroller. Black and sleek with different pockets and buttons. I wouldn't even know where to begin with that thing.

"Um. You know, I'll need to think about it."

Rita points at me. "Blood sugar. Low blood sugar. Go get some lunch and come back. We're open until five. I'll hold onto your cart."

Keifer looks to me, concern plastered over his face. "Are you hungry, Dar?"

Now that they both mention it..." I could eat."

"Alright. Then let's go grab something." Keifer thanks Rita for all her help before we go out into the parking lot. "Hey, are you alright?"

I feel my face tighten. "Yeah, I'm just feeling funny."

"Funny?"

"I don't know. Let's just get something to eat."

Keifer doesn't push any harder, giving my emotions a wide berth due to my condition. He doesn't argue a bit when I say I'm craving fried food. We opt for a drive-thru nearby. My eyes are bigger than my stomach, or maybe it's the reverse. I'm not just hungry. I'm starving.

"Wow, why didn't you say anything?" he asks as he pulls the car forward.

"I didn't realize I was so hungry until just now," I say sheepishly.

Keifer smiles and starts tapping on the steering wheel as we wait our turn in the drive-thru line. "That was funny, wasn't it? That she thought we were together."

Funny isn't how I'd describe it. Does it seem like a joke to him? "Yeah. It was."

"I guess I don't blame her. We are walking around shopping for baby stuff, after all."

"Sure, I guess it's natural to assume."

Keifer glances over at me and I at him. We both look away.

"You're the one who played along," I say dryly.

"Me?! You're the one who said thank you!"

"Yeah! I thought I'd say thank you and then we could move on, but you and Rita are best friends or whatever."

Finally, we make it up to the window. Our conversation is on pause as Keifer pays and retrieves our food. As soon as I get the bag in my lap, I grab a handful of fries and stuff them in my mouth. "Mmm..."

Keifer chuckles. "Hitting the spot?"

"Yes, dear god," I say through a mouthful of food.

Keifer parks the car and we eat, staring out the front window at the road. "So, are you jealous of me and Rita?"

"What?!"

"You heard me!"

He's definitely joking, but I can't help taking him seriously. "*No*. What makes you think that?"

"I don't know. You sound jealous."

"I'm not," I say all too forcefully. "Besides. It's none of my business if post-menopausal women are your type."

"*Dara*."

I look at him.

"*You're* my type."

I stop mid chew. "Really?"

"Obviously," he says with a gesture toward my stomach.

I swallow, hard, since the food is only half chewed. "Oh."

Keifer laughs. "Why are you acting surprised?"

"I don't know. I mean, I know we have chemistry, but you know, the first time we were drunk and the other times we were angry which is *basically* like being drunk, so..."

His eyes fall to my lips. I should wipe them off in case there's any granules of salt left behind, but I'm trapped under the weight of his jade eyes.

"Goddammit," he mutters, pushing himself further into the driver's side door.

"What? What's wrong?"

"I don't want to fuck this up, Dara."

"What do you mean?"

"I *mean*..." Keifer runs his hands over his face. "I really would love to kiss you, but I'm afraid that would fuck this all up. I'm trying to take it slow and make sure we actually know each other and know if something would work before either of us do anything..."

I smile meekly. "Stupid?"

"Yeah. Stupid."

He laughs sadly and looks down into his lap.

So, now I know. There's something there. A feeling. It's new and it's growing. It could so easily break, ruin everything if we move too fast.

I'm alright with moving slow if I know we're moving at all.

And with Keifer, it sounds like I'm moving somewhere.

I reach out across the console and take his hand in mine. He allows me to pull his hand into my lap. I trace my thumb back and forth softly over his skin.

Neither of us speaks. We can't do more than this. Not yet.

But hopefully very soon, we can explore the idea that we won't only love the baby. We may love each other too.

I take a deep breath. "I have an ultrasound tomorrow."

Keifer glances my way, raising an eyebrow.

"You know, I'm a little behind on all that, but, um... I should be finding out the gender, and if you wanted to come, you could."

The corner of his mouth twitches into a smile and then disappears. "Do you want me to come?"

I'm quiet, resisting the urge to say vehemently, *Yes. I don't just want you to come. I need you to.*

"Because you don't just have to invite me to be nice, Dara. I know it's probably personal."

"I'm not, Keifer. And it *is* personal, for the both of us, so yes, I want you to come."

A moment. "Really?"

"Yes. But only if you want to. I get it if it feels like a lot is happening too fast. Plus, you have work, and it's right in the middle of the afternoon, so I..."

Keifer reaches toward me. My heart starts to beat wildly, not knowing what he's about to do. He captures my chin between his fingers, making sure my eyes are locked in his. "I'll be there."

I could kiss him right now. He's so close. I touch his wrist to let him know his closeness is welcomed.

Suddenly, he's leaning toward me. But as soon as the thought crosses my mind that he'll kiss me, he diverts his lips to my cheek. A soft, chaste kiss against my skin.

"Was that alright?" he asks.

"More than."

Keifer retreats, and though I want more, I remember what he said. We're taking things slow. If that means a small kiss to the cheek is all I get for now, so be it.

Because I'm hopeful there'll be much, much more in our future.

I haven't been able to focus on work all day. I'm just scrolling through emails and on my phone, trying to pass the time until one o'clock. That's when Dara's meeting me to go to her ultrasound.

I'm excited and nervous, all at once, making me a buzzing ball of anxiety and energy which unfortunately is noticeable to my brothers and dad.

"Too much coffee today?"

I raise my gaze from my salad to Dad across the table. "Huh?"

"Your hand's shaking."

He's right. Romaine lettuce trembles from my fork, my grip unsteady. "Uh. Yeah. Way too much espresso."

"You have to start keeping an eye on that, Keifer," Jarred says.

We're sitting around a table in one of the conference tables sharing lunch, which is a much rarer occurrence these days. Jarred and Dad have started using their breaks to call home and check in with their wives and babies, leaving

Oliver and me to our own devices. More often than not, the two of us opt just to fuck around on our own.

I have a sudden realization. Am I going to turn into Dad and Jarred on my breaks? Rushing off so I can talk on the phone with Dara to check in about the baby? About her?

"I know you still feel young because you're in your twenties, but the sooner you get bad habits in check, the sooner the good habits form," Jarred continues.

Oliver rolls his eyes. "God, you sound so old, Jarred."

"When you're a father, you'll understand," Dad pipes up.

Jarred nods adamantly.

I hate this conversation. The kids and their wives come first in every choice Dad and Jarred make. That's my future too, I guess. That was what Dara and I agreed to. Every choice we make, our baby has to come first. Which means I'm going to be consulting with Dara for the rest of my life, what I can and can't do. That thought makes me shiver. What if I want to live somewhere else? What if we want to expand Hawthorn to the west coast and I'm leading the charge? What if things don't work out with Dara and me and I meet someone else? And what if she's French or Italian and wants to live in her home country?!

Okay, these are *a lot* of ifs. And the baby is not an if but a when.

And Dara...

Dara's still an if. I haven't figured out if she's a when yet. Not for lack of wanting. I haven't stopped wanting Dara since the moment I met her. But just because we're having a baby together doesn't mean a relationship is implicit. Sure, I'm willing to try, but there's a lot to get figured out before then.

"Keif," Oliver's voice breaks through my spiraling thoughts.

"What?"

"You want to come out with me and Trev tomorrow night?"

I raise an eyebrow. "You guys playing darts again?"

"Well, yeah. It's a tournament."

"It's an ongoing rivalry at best. Besides, you're both shit at darts." I glance over at Dad and Jarred for support, but they're gawking at Dad's phone, no doubt at a new picture of Ivy.

Oliver rolls his eyes. "Do you want in or not?"

I shake my head. Dara might need me. "Pass."

"Damn, you're just as boring as the dads."

Shit. Yeah. Maybe I am. After all, my first thought when it came to going out was Dara. What if she needs me to make her dinner or run out and grab something for her? Maybe once we know the gender, we'll become obsessed with planning the nursery.

"If you change your mind, let me know. I'm getting tired of Trevor being a sad sack all the time. I need someone to play off of so that the mood is upbeat and not depressing."

I sigh. "He's still on the Rowan thing?"

"The she who shall not be named thing, you mean? Yeah. It's rough. The guy is barely eating, barely sleeping, but trying to pretend he's fine. Won't talk about it. But when we go out, he starts dissociating and I have to snap him out of it."

"That sucks."

Oliver rolls his eyes. "Tell me about it. We gotta get him laid. And get you laid while we're at it."

Me, getting laid? I bristle at the thought. If it's not Dara,

I'm not sure I want it. "What about you, Oliver? You don't want to get laid?"

"Eh. You know me. I'm better in the wingman role. Once a girl starts talking to me, I get all tongue-tied and embarrassed."

I smile. My older brother is the biggest of us all, arguably the most sought after by the ladies, and doesn't know what to do with all the attention. I don't think he's ever even had a girlfriend. If he did, he didn't say anything.

Suddenly, my smart watch buzzes on my wrist. *Eve.* That's what I have Dara as in my contact list. Then I don't have to worry about anyone seeing the name on my phone.

Here a little early :)

Shit. I told Dara to meet me at Hawthorn at one. If anything, I expected her to be late with how public transportation is running these days. Not *early.* "I gotta go."

"You've barely eaten anything," Dad says, gesturing to the mostly full container of salad in front of me.

"Forgot I have a dentist appointment," I say. "I'll be out for a couple hours."

The guys all gawk at me in confusion. We're all usually pretty good about letting each other know when we're going to be out of the office. For the most part, things are flexible, and we can pick up the slack.

"Sorry. I should have mentioned it, but it slipped my mind."

Though Oliver and Jarred look miffed at best, it's Dad who seems to be trying to see through me. He's always been good at knowing when we're lying. That's what having three boys does to you. I think he picked up that trick from Mom. "Okay. Just a cleaning or what?" he asks, crossing his arms over his chest.

"Uhm yeah. Have to get my pearly whites all pearly white. You know how it goes. Anyway. Be back later, bye!"

I rush out of the conference room, ignoring what a terrible exit that was. I'm definitely going to get questions about it later. For now, though, the only thing on my mind is getting to Dara.

I hurry to the elevator and head down to the lobby.

Dara is waiting outside on the corner. God, she's a vision. Her blonde tresses look like gold. She wears a loose blouse tucked into a long skirt. It's getting impossible to hide the fact she's pregnant, and given how Chicago is heating up for summer, it's probably getting uncomfortable to continue wearing big sweaters.

When she sees me, she smiles. It might be a little dangerous that she's meeting me at my work, but for all anyone knows, she's just my good friend. My good, pregnant, beautiful friend.

We greet each other and walk to the parking garage. "You got here early."

"I'm sorry, I hope I didn't interrupt anything. I could have waited."

"Oh, no, it's okay. I was just having lunch with the guys. I needed an out."

We make it to the car, get all buckled in, and then it hits me. it's really happening. I'm going to see my baby. I don't think I've felt this giddy in years.

"You ready?" Dara asks, resting a hand on her belly.

I can't help myself. "Did I tell you how beautiful you look?"

She blushes and looks away, shaking her head. The smile on her lips shows me that the compliment wasn't unwelcome.

I smile triumphantly. "Let's go."

Even though we arrive early at the doctor's office, we're kept waiting until ten minutes after our scheduled time. My excitement and confidence have worn off entirely by the time we're called in. In the waiting room, I couldn't help looking around at all the other people there. Women in various states of pregnancy, some alone, some with their partners. Others with tiny babies in their arms coming for postpartum checkups.

Dara sensed my nerves and kept her hand on my elbow for the entire wait.

Now, in the examination room, we are greeted by an ultrasound technician, Hannah. She's young and has a buzzed haircut dyed blue.

"How are you two doing today?" she says, chewing a piece of gum as she speaks.

"Good. Nervous," Dara says.

"Is this daddy?" Hannah asks, looking my way.

My eyebrows jump. "Um. Yeah. That's me." The word daddy hitting me square in the chest.

Hannah claps her hands together. "Exciting! Alright, let's get started and take a look at this baby."

I help Dara onto the examination table. I hope she doesn't notice how clammy my hands are. Once she's laid back, she pulls up her loose shirt, revealing her stomach. I haven't seen it bare yet and my attention is rapt. The pale skin of her belly looks milky smooth except for her belly button that is starting to stretch the slightest bit. Dara feels my eyes on her and looks up at me. "You okay?"

I sit on a stool that Hanna placed next to the table for me. "Y-yes. Sorry."

"Oh, he's nervous. That's natural." Hannah squeezes some sort of gel onto Dara's stomach.

"Are you nervous, Keifer?"

Her smile is so inviting, I can't help but be honest. "Yes. But in a good way."

Dara takes my hand and holds it up against her chest.

"Okay, let's get started." Hanna starts to slide the wand thingy across Dara's stomach, watching the screen that's turned all the way in her direction.

Every second that goes by heightens my anxiety. Why is it taking so long? What's she trying to find?

"There's the heartbeat..."

A thrumming, grainy beat can be heard all around the room. A heartbeat. So fast. Should it be this fast?

"And there's the baby!" Hannah turns the screen to face us.

Though the image is grainy, it's very obvious the outline of a baby. I can make out the arms and legs. The nose. My eyes immediately fill with tears.

"Perfect size for five months. Probably in a pretty high percentile for weight given how you're carrying right now."

I'm transfixed on the screen. It's just hitting me how real this is. It's not just an abstract idea. That's a baby. *My* baby.

Dara touches my cheek and wipes a tear away from under my eye. "Are you okay?"

"Yeah, yeah. I'm happy. It's happy tears. I promise." I brush some hair out of her face. Emotion is swelling inside me. I can't help but kiss her forehead.

"You two are so cute!" Hannah chirps. "Okay. Did you want to find out the gender today?"

"Yeah, I think so."

Hannah grins, "Do you have a guess?"

I laugh, wiping a few more tears away with my sleeve. "No, no. Just want a healthy baby. That's all that matters."

She moves the wand thingy slightly. "Mhm. Uh huh. Well, there's no doubt about it, that's a little baby boy."

"I knew it!" Dara says excitedly.

I'm about to kiss her again, for real this time, when the technician gasps. "Hold on." She turns the screen away from us and starts moving that wand all around Dara's belly.

Dara and I both watch her intently. "Is something wrong?" I ask, although I'm not sure if it comes out much louder than a whisper.

"No, not wrong, not..." Hannah peeks out from behind the screen. "You haven't been told you're having twins yet, have you?"

Silence. I feel numb.

One baby. That's already been a lot to wrap my mind around. Two babies? That's a whole other ball game.

"N-no..." Dara squeaks.

Hannah doesn't seem to notice how the air has left the room. She shrugs and smiles. "Double the baby, double the fun!" She turns the screen back to face us. "Your second little one's been hiding! See right there you can spy another leg, another arm and if you look right here..." She gestures to a grainy outline that I can barely see because my vision is blurred. "Twin boys!"

Not just twins but twin boys. Dear god. This is a lot to take in.

"Also probably why you're carrying so large already."

"How did this...how didn't I know?" Dara asks, just as stunned as I am.

"Well, it seems like your babies are sharing a placenta, which means they're sharing an amniotic sac. That means they're *really* up close and personal with each other. Easier for a twin to hide. But not forever!" Hannah giggles. "So, you'll want some prints, right?"

The rest of the appointment feels like I'm trapped in a fog. I was ready for one baby, not two.

Dara and I can barely look at each other. Somehow, we both know that this has changed...everything.

But has it? They're still both my children. My *sons*.

Making things work between me and Dara with one baby seemed possible.

I don't know what's possible anymore.

At the end of the appointment, we get several copies of the ultrasounds. I tuck them right into my suit jacket. I can't bear to look at them again. Not now.

I feel like a horrible person, but it's too much. I should be thrilled, ecstatic that by some genetic stroke of luck we have managed to get two babies in one go.

All I feel is dread.

From the moment the technician said twins, I knew I'd lost him.

His eyes that had been trembling with tears suddenly glazed over, his hand went limp in mine, he retreated somewhere far away. Unreachable. From the way he turned pale as a sheet, I thought he might pass out.

Thank god he didn't just walk out of the examination room. It would have been dramatic, but for a minute there, I wasn't sure.

It certainly didn't help that Hannah, the technician, was bubbly beyond compare. "Double the babies, double the fun!" Those are clearly the words of someone who has never been pregnant and isn't looking down the barrel of eighteen years of being a parent.

Or should I say a *lifetime* of it. My whole life is about to change. I'm about to step into a role that I will never step out of. And I'm only twenty-five.

Two whole babies. Damn, when I screw up, I do it pretty spectacularly, don't I?

To make matters worse, I'm so upset that I'm not

jumping for joy. I'd managed to find the happiness and excitement from my pregnancy pretty soon after finding out. Now I feel like I have to find that joy all over again. Do I have enough love to give two babies when I still feel like such a kid myself? Can my body handle growing two babies? Pushing two out? Dear god, I don't even want to think about what labor will be like or how big I'll get.

On top of all of that, I'm going to have to completely rework my expenses and debt payments. Double the babies also means double the expenses, *Hannah*. Two of everything. Keifer was comfortable footing the bill for one baby, but he never consented to two.

Keifer and I have not uttered a single word to each other. We just left the office and got into the car. Wordlessly, he decided on a destination and drove off. I realized, after a few moments, we were headed up to Mayfair.

Home. Our home. The home of our unborn children.

Child*ren*. The word makes me lightheaded.

As we drive, the baby – *one* of the babies flutters. It's become more and more noticeable to me when they move. I touch my belly tenderly. They probably can feel how stressed I am. I bite back tears. I would never want a child of mine to feel unwanted, but this is so fucked.

All of this from one night of blissed out sex. Doesn't matter how good it felt. The ups and downs of pregnancy do not make it worth it.

I keep my gaze focused out the window. I could just ask Keifer how he's feeling, but I can't bring myself to utter a single word. I know that if it is anything close to what I'm feeling, this may be it for us. And I want to delay that knowledge for a little while longer. Denial is my friend. Because I can't deal with all the what ifs that are haunting me right now.

What if he drops me off at home and drives off into the sunset, never to be seen again? What if he's mad at me and yells at me for being too fucking fertile or something? What if he takes it all back? Casts me aside and disowns his children?

What if he thinks he's made a mistake? What if he hates me now?

Any and all of these situations would break my heart.

It is the *longest* car ride of my life. When we turn onto the cul-de-sac, I'm both relieved and terrified. We have to speak now, don't we?

But what will we say?

Keifer parks the truck and turns the keys in the ignition. We sit there in silence, our eyes downcast. I don't know if I should wait for him to speak or if I should say something first. Apologize maybe.

"I didn't–"

"That was–"

Naturally, we speak simultaneously and then seal our mouths shut.

I realize I'm errantly stroking my belly. Regardless of the mental anguish the idea of twins has caused, I'm still their mother. My maternal instinct is strong. And they are my priority.

"I had no idea," I finally say, breaking the silence.

Keifer doesn't reply.

"I promise, you have to believe me."

"I do. I know you're not lying, Dara."

I nod. "Good."

"That was a lot. For both of us, I think," he says in a small voice.

"Yeah. It was." My mouth curdles into a frown. "I'm sorry."

Keifer sighs. "Don't be sorry."

"It's my fault."

"It's not."

"Yes, it is."

"Dara, we're both responsible. That's biology. It's how it works."

I shake my head. "No. It's mine. My body didn't have to go and fucking make twins. It could have just been normal and made one accidental baby. But *no*, it had to double down and really just fuck everything up." By the end, I'm nearly yelling.

"You had no control over that, Dara."

"Well, I should! I should have control over something! I've never had control over one goddamn thing. Not my parents, not the insurance companies, not my own fucking body! When do I get to be in control and decide something? *Anything*."

Tears are rolling down my face. I'm so angry at the world.

To my surprise, Keifer touches my shoulder. He rubs it gently. But he won't look at me. His gaze is steadily out the window. "You could have chosen not to have the baby."

My eyes widen. "What did you say?"

"I just...that's a decision you could have made."

"Is that what you wish I had done? That I'd gotten rid of it. Of them?"

"No! No..." I'm not convinced. "I'm just saying you had more of a choice than you think, Dara."

I shake his hand off my shoulder. "Don't talk to me about choice. You can do anything you want. You have all the money in the world. You could jet off to Greece tomorrow and never speak to me again."

"I'm not going to do that!"

"No? Are you sure? Because you just implied I could have gotten rid of the baby – the *babies* – and then we wouldn't be in this mess. Right? That's all my fault, isn't it?"

Keifer shakes his head. "You're putting so many words in my mouth."

"It's what you *said*."

He goes silent. My heart throbs. I want better from him. I know he's scared, but I thought maybe we could be scared together rather than pushing each other away.

I thought we were falling for each other. I should have known better than to think that was a commitment. It was just a dream. Not something I should have believed.

"You're making me sound like I said you *should* have done that. And that's not what I said at all."

"Then why even bring it up that I had a choice in the matter? Have *you* ever carried a baby? Do you know what it feels like to know you're creating something that relies on you? That you're supposed to love? No. You don't. You never will."

"Yeah, Dara, you're right. I'll never know that. All I will know is the terror of finding out that someone is carrying my baby and having to figure out how to be a man about it!"

I go rigid. "Well, please, don't go out of your way to 'be a man' on my account." I push the door open and storm toward my house.

Keifer follows. "Dara, come on! Don't walk away from me!"

"No, I get it now, Keifer. You're surrounded by men who step up and the only reason you even agreed to be a part of the baby's life in the first place is so that your pride isn't impacted because god forbid you show the world how much of a coward you really are." I don't know where all this anger is coming from. But I can't seem to be able to stifle it.

"The reason I wanted to step up is because I wanted to step up. That's it." His willingness to fight fades from his eyes. Cold green eyes turning sad. "That's it. I promise."

My head is pounding.

"Do you really think that I–"

"No!" my voice breaks. "I'm just so mad that everything keeps changing!"

Keifer watches me. "I get it. Me too."

I fold my hands over my eyes, weeping. "What are we going to do?"

"I don't know."

That answer makes it clear to me that I cannot count on "we". I need to be prepared for the question to be, *What am I going to do?* I gain my composure as best I can, folding my arms across my chest and surveying the cul-de-sac. This place that has become my home, my safe haven, now feels like a prison.

"I think we both should take some time to think about it," Keifer says softly, but I can hear every word as if he's whispering it right in my ear.

I nod. "Yeah. I think so too." I'd much rather us think about it together, figure it out *together*.

"I just need some time to process. I'm not running away to Greece or anything. Alright?"

I don't believe him entirely, but I try to smile. "Okay."

Keifer starts to go back to the truck. "Please take care of yourself, okay? You need to be eating really well and resting and–"

"Keifer?"

He swallows the rest of his words.

"I know what I have to do, okay? I can take care of

myself." That last sentence is meant to cut him to the quick. I've taken care of myself for five years now. There's no reason I need someone to start trying to take care of me now.

Even if I'm about to have two babies.

He nods as if I've knocked him on the head. "Okay...okay."

I watch him get back into the truck and drive away. I don't look away for a second. If he looks in the rearview mirror, I want him to remember how he abandoned the woman carrying his children like this when she needed him.

It dawns on me. I need him. I want him. I've been falling for him. I was so close to loving him.

And now, I have no idea if I even knew him.

I go inside and stand in the hallway, not knowing what to do next. I'm hungry and could definitely eat. And I'm tired, so I could definitely take a nap.

And I'm alone.

Physically, alone. Mentally...still alone. The only person I've been able to be entirely honest with about my pregnancy just left.

But there is one other person. Someone I've been pushing away as I've gotten closer to Keifer, who knows about my pregnancy, except for the one crucial detail of paternity.

I pull out my phone and call Rye.

She picks up on the first ring. "Dara! I haven't heard from you in a week! What's going on?"

"Can you come over?"

A moment. "What's going on, Dara? Is everything alright with the baby?"

The tears spill out again. "Twins."

"What?"

"It's twins. I just had an ultrasound."

Rye gasps. "Oh my god, Dara. H-how do you feel?"

"Terrible. I'm so scared. I'm panicking."

I can hear her rushing around. "Okay, okay. I'll get Ivy ready, and we'll come over now. Just hold tight."

The babies flutter again. Despite all the panic, feeling them move still brings a smile to my face.

"Have you eaten? I'll pick something up."

"I'm starving. Anything. Just no–"

"Onions. I got you."

I can't believe I've pushed her away the past few weeks. I've disdained her for all her offers of help, hidden the truth from her, done everything but let my friend be my friend.

"Okay, you just rest. Lay down, put something fun on TV, and I'll be there as soon as I–"

I have to tell her. "Rye."

"What? What's wrong?"

Fuck secrets I'm tired of them. "I have to tell you something."

"...okay."

"And you can't be mad when I tell you."

"Never, Dara."

I go to the living room and look out the window at Keifer's empty house. "I need to tell you who the father is."

TWENTY-SIX

KEIFER

The door flies open. Oliver is on the other side, hair sticking out in all directions, squinting at me.

"Hey bro!" I clap him on the arm and then hold up a bottle of champagne. "I brought stuff for mimosas."

Oliver frowns. "What time is it?"

"Nine!"

"It's Saturday."

"I know! That's why we gotta get started on sloppy Saturday, pronto!" I push past him into the apartment. Oliver's pad has always been the trendiest between the three of us. It's in a new complex in Fulton Market and has all the bells and whistles. There are so many buttons that all do different random things. I've never understood the appeal of having a house with buttons, but that's Oliver. He's been obsessed with new tech since he was a kid. It only makes sense he's the chief security officer at Hawthorn.

Another thing about his apartment is that it's incredibly *clean*. He's a fucking neat freak. It looks like a robot lives here, not a bachelor. His kitchen is spotless.

"You have any orange juice?" I ask as I open the fridge.

Organized with labels and everything. Jesus Christ, when does this guy loosen up?

"Should be some in there."

I grab the orange juice off the shelf and start to pour two drinks. I'm buzzing with excitement. After leaving the cul-de-sac the night before, I texted Oliver that I was in for a Saturday with the boys. His response was just one word: *Sick.*

I took it upon myself to decide the time.

"I didn't expect you so early, man," Oliver says through a yawn.

"Yeah, well, here I am, and –" I grab my glass. "— bottoms up."

Oliver takes his uneasily and takes a sip. "Man, we're too old to start drinking this early."

I laugh. This guy doesn't even have kids and he's saying he's too old for a little day drinking. Wait till he's in my shoes.

I've been shaken up since getting the news that Dara's pregnant with twins yesterday. I'm so pissed at myself for the way I handled it, but I was in shock. She has had all the time in the world to adjust to the idea of having a baby. I found out what feels like yesterday that I'm about to be a dad, and literally yesterday I'm dropped another bomb. I was struggling but coming to terms with having a kid, and now I have to think about having two?

I needed some time to myself. I ended up spending the night at a hotel to clear my head.

Today, though, is for the boys.

I don't yet know how I feel about twins. Twin *boys.* God. Three boys of different ages was hard enough on my parents. Two at the same time? I can't even fathom what kind of hell that's going to be.

That's not what I think, though. Not really. I feel like a guy in my shoes, in his late-ish twenties, handsome, with lots of money, would be lamenting his freedom being snatched away by an unexpected pregnancy.

But at my core, I know that's not how I feel. The past two weeks with Dara, developing our relationship, thinking about how we're going to coparent our child, have been...amazing.

Child turning to child*ren* shouldn't throw a whole wrench into everything we've built, should it?

I'm just so fucking scared.

No thinking about the kid thing today. That's the rule.

I down my mimosa in a couple gulps and pour another. "When's Trevor coming over?"

"Jeez, you good, dude? You're drinking that like it's juice."

I chuckle as I pour the orange juice. "It *is* juice."

Oliver rolls his eyes. "You know what I mean."

"I'm just in the mood to party. You said that's what you guys were gonna do, right?"

"I said we were going to throw darts, not be hospitalized."

"Since when did you get all high and mighty about drinking? It's champagne. Get a grip. Besides, we'll order some breakfast, get those carbs in. I'll hydrate with some water. We'll be good all day."

I know Oliver can't resist an invitation like that. It's logical and maximizes the fun. My older brother might be measured and cautious in a lot of things, but he knows how to get down. "I'll text him now."

"Perfect."

June is baseball season. And being northside babies, we're Cubs fans all the way. Now, given our money and reputation, it's easy to get a box seat, do the whole luxury thing.

But where's the fun in that?

When we were kids, Dad would take the three of us to sit in the bleachers. This is before Hawthorn really took off, so money was still something to be spent wisely and sparsely. We'd load up on water and sunscreen and eat shitty hotdogs in the blistering summer sun.

Best memories ever.

So, that's what we're emulating today. Except instead of water, it's shitty, overpriced beer.

"Here, bro." Trevor passes me another can of beer as he takes his seat next to me on the bleacher.

The smell of crappy beer stings my nose as I sip it. "Mmgh. I think I'm gonna be sick."

"Well, aim that way if you are," Oliver says, nudging me on the shoulder toward Trevor.

Trevor pushes me back. I'm wobbly, feeling like a ping pong ball being volleyed back and forth. "Damn, man, maybe you should slow down? You've been going hard since this morning."

Trevor arrived at Oliver's shortly after he sent the text. We finished up the champagne and then started in on some hard seltzers in the fridge while we played a few rounds of Call of Duty.

After a hearty breakfast, we went to River North to a sports bar to watch the game, started in on some beers and then realized we could be *at* the game. So, we got our asses up to Wrigleyville and made it by the fifth inning.

I'm starting to feel queasy. Not sure if it's all the alcohol, the shitty hotdogs that have been sitting out in the sun, or the nerves still bubbling in my gut.

We watch the next player go up to home plate and wind up his bat. It's a home game, so the crowd's attention is rapt. This is the Cubs' star player. He's just been on a streak of homeruns and grand slams, so everyone in the bleachers is on the edge of their seats, excited at the possibly of catching a ball.

Unfortunately, my stomach doesn't seem to be able to handle it.

I groan. "I gotta go to the bathroom."

"Get the hell outta here, man! Go!" Oliver smacks me in the ass as I stand up.

The people sitting behind us yell at me to get out of the way and I rush up the stairs as fast as I can, hoping I can hold it down until I get to the bathroom.

I sprint through the stadium, hearing the crowd gasp and then start cheering. *Fuck, can't believe I missed it.*

Doesn't matter, though, because the excitement surely would have made me lose my lunch.

I make it to the bathroom just in time, sinking to my knees. I retch into the toilet, acid burning my throat. My head pounds. I don't even notice how bad it probably smells in here. I don't care. I just gotta get everything out.

I should have listened to Oliver, but I've been spiraling inside without anyone to talk to about what's going on.

"Don't think about it..." I whisper.

My stomach heaves again in response, but nothing comes up.

"Fuck..."

I flush the toilet and wipe my mouth with the back of my hand. Damn, I really can't drink like I used to. I used to be able to go all day and night without losing it.

I sit in the stall for a few minutes. The floor sticky with beer and piss, but I don't care.

Shockingly, just because I decided *not* to think about the babies doesn't mean I'm not thinking about them. Thinking about Dara.

I feel like such a piece of shit for how things went down. On top of it, I feel like even more of a piece of shit for going out and getting trashed before it's even five o'clock. Maybe I'm not ready. Maybe I should just...run away.

Women scare me. The things they're capable of. The passion with which they do things. Dara's carrying two babies. My babies. What did I do? I just fucking came in her. That's so dumb. She can't go out and get fucked up and run away from the situation. It's with her all the time.

I'm still a kid. She's younger than me, but I'm the kid. The immature one.

She deserves better.

"Hey man, you okay?"

I sit up suddenly. Outside mine stall is a man with a deep voice. All I can see of him are his sneakers. "Uh. Yeah. Yeah. Sorry."

"You're good. Just wanna make sure we don't need to get you some help or anything."

I get to my feet quickly and open the stall door. There's a guy just a bit shorter than me but not much older with a spattering of dark facial hair. He's bald and looks tired, but happy. "Just overdid it."

"I hear that. It's easy to do. Be careful, though, okay? Your boys need you!" He punches me on the arm.

It's like he's reading my mind. I know he's just making a statement in jest, assuming I'm here with some guy friends. But I can't help but think about *my* boys.

"Will do. Thanks for checking on me."

"Sure thing." The guy nods and walks off.

I wash my hands and face, rinse my mouth out while I'm at it. And then I'm off to the bleachers again.

However, when I leave the bathroom, I catch sight of my kind stranger. He's standing with two young boys. They remind me of Jarred and Oliver. Close in age, always sort of picking on each other, but lovingly so.

They wait together. The boys start chasing each other around and through Dad's legs and Dad's a good sport, but suddenly, he picks one of them and lifts him into the air. The stadium hall is alit with the little boy's laughter.

Then, from the woman's bathroom, the mother emerges. At least, I'm assuming she's the mother, by the way the other boy's face lights up and how he rushes over to her as if she's been gone eons rather than just a few minutes. They walk hand in hand back to the rest of their family. And with a delicate, casualness, the mother and father share a small kiss.

It's not overly romantic or anything. It's normal for them. It's their everyday. And for some reason, to me, it's one of the most beautiful sights.

Everywhere I look, I see kids, couples, happiness. It's getting annoying. Here I am, with my boys, supposed to be having the time of my fucking life and I'm thinking about...

Dara.

I could have all that.

I'm just not sure I deserve it.

"I just need you to know I'm really pissed at you."

I stare at Rye. She's standing just past the threshold of my house. Alone.

After I told her who the father was last night, she understandably decided not to come over. She didn't ask any questions, but I could hear the hurt in her voice.

"I need some time to process this."

It cut what little was left of my heart in two, after Keifer's rejection. "I understand. Just, please don't say anything to Ash."

Rye didn't respond to my request. Just said, "I'll be by tomorrow," and hung up.

Now, she's here. And she's holding the food she promised to bring last night. And her expression is that odd parental mixture of love and disappointment. I can almost hear her say, *I thought you were better than this.*

"You want to come in and eat?"

Rye shoves the food into my arms and bumps past me as she goes inside.

Well, that's a start.

"You have a lot of explaining to do, Dara."

"Okay, Mom."

"Stop it! I'm not your mom!"

"Then why do I have to explain anything to you?" I scoff and open the bag of greasy food, fishing out a fry.

"Because I'm your best friend! And you've been hiding this from me!"

I swallow the fry down and then shake my head. "You know it's kind of a conflict of interests. I didn't want it getting complicated for you."

"You're always anticipating how people will feel before you even let them tell you how they feel. It's really annoying."

"Ooookay, this is gonna be brutal. Let me sit."

I follow her into the living room and sit awkwardly in one of the armchairs. Now that I know I'm pregnant with twins, I'm really leaning into the pregnant thing. It's like I'm allowing myself to actually feel as tired as I am. Makes sense. I'm bigger than a regular pregnancy would be. Growing two babies takes twice the energy.

Rye notices how heavily I sit and her anger breaks for a moment. "How are you feeling?"

"Pregnant."

"Yeah. I get it."

I can't help but laugh. It was supposed to be a jab, but of course she gets it. She's been pregnant too. "I hope you didn't expect to eat any of this, because this is hardly enough for me."

Rye smiles sadly. "No, I ate already. But I can go back if you need more."

"I'm joking, Rye."

"Right."

She sits on the edge of the couch, her fingers dancing on her leg. "Does he know?"

"Yeah. He found out when I was in the hospital."

"Jeez, you were hiding it from him that long?"

I gnaw on a chicken nugget. "You remember that thing you just said about anticipating people's reactions and not giving them a chance to actually react. It was kinda one of those things. Besides, he was being kind of a jerk, if you remember."

"So...how did he take it?"

I sigh. I've been playing the events of the past few weeks on repeat. The way Keifer and I just seemed to so easily bond together like magnets. Inevitable and tight. Our creation pulling us together. Each positive memory has been part of my case as to why I want Keifer. And somehow in one go, he ruined the whole thing. "It was good. At first. He wanted to be involved. Which was nice."

"I bet."

"And yesterday, he went with me to the ultrasound. And we both panicked. Really bad. And it got really bad."

"Oh, Dara, I'm sorry."

"It's okay." My eyes fill with tears.

"I should've been here. I should've come to see you. I was just so hurt."

I nod heavily. "I understand."

"But that doesn't excuse...that must have been so hard." Her eyes are filling with tears too.

"You can't cry. I'm about to cry."

Somehow, she beats me to the punch and the tears start streaming down her face. *Typical.* "I'm sorry! I'm trying not to. I just feel bad."

"Well, build a bridge and get over it. You're here now. So, let's talk."

Rye wipes her face and nods. "Okay. How did it happen?"

I explain everything, leaving out the nasty details so that Rye can face her husband with all this information. "That reminds me, did you tell Ash?"

She shakes her head. "Of course not, Dara."

"What do you mean 'of course'? He's your husband."

"Yeah, but just because he's my husband doesn't means he's the only person who I need to be trustworthy to. Right?"

I beam. "Wow, seriously?"

"Obviously. Is that why you didn't tell me?"

I nod. "I was scared."

Rye's quiet for a moment. "I wish you had."

"Me too."

We sit in silence. I eat and Rye watches. We're both thinking so many things. The room is echoing with things unsaid. But I gotta focus on getting as many calories down as possible so I don't pass out. Once I'm all finished with my food, I fold up the bag and look at Rye.

Her eyes harden on me. "How are *you* feeling about the twin thing?"

"Terrified."

"He's not gonna leave you high and dry."

"How do you know?"

"I don't, but –"

"Seriously, Rye. How do you know that?"

Rye shrugs. "I don't! You're right. I can't say that for sure, without a doubt Keifer is a good guy. I want to. I love him. But you know...people are strange. Guys are strange." She cocks her head. "But...if his family's track record says anything–"

"Oh god."

"I'm just saying. Ash stepped up. Jarred stepped up." Rye smiles and comes over to me, sitting on the arm of my chair. "Actually, if you think about it, Ash stepped up twice. Those kids wouldn't probably have been born if he hadn't married Rose."

Damn. She's right. There's like ancestral karma here.

"You think that Keifer's just gonna break this long line of stepping up? No way."

I lean my head in my hand and look off across the living room. I'm picturing so many things. A Christmas tree. Two little ones buried in wrapping paper. Toys everywhere. Keifer chasing after them. I can hear the laughter and smell the coffee and baby powder.

Man, that seems awesome.

"It's not just about Keifer stepping up," I say softly.

Rye runs her hand through my hair. "I know, honey."

"I think I really like him." My voice breaks saying those words and the tears I held back for Rye's sake start to tumble down my face. "I think I might love him."

Rye wraps her arms around me. "Shhhh, honey. It's okay. Shhhh..."

I weep into her arms. This feels harder than any rejection I've felt before. It's not just me. But my babies. The ones I chose to have. Keifer was right about that, even if I disdained his pointing out.

I chose this.

But for him to walk away from me, means he is walking away from our family.

And I really wanted that now that I've seen the possibility.

The worst part is that I don't know if I've been rejected yet, though it feels like it.

"We don't know anything for a fact about what Keifer is

feeling or what he's gonna do," Rye says. She gently turns my face toward hers. "So that means, we have to figure out what we can control. You have to let me help you, Dara."

Ugh...help me? Do I even deserve it at this point?

"I know what you're thinking and don't even think for a second that you can–"

"Alright." It just comes out. And my body feels so light despite getting heavier by the day. "Help me, Rye."

Rye grins. "You won't regret it."

After a nap and a big dinner, I've been able to rally to make it out for darts with Trevor and Oliver.

And now that I'm more aware of what's going on, I get what Oliver means.

Trevor's down *bad*.

"I feel like I need to just start over. You know?" Trevor says, looking off into the distance with glazed over eyes.

I throw another dart at board. "Sure, man. That's what you're doing."

"No, no. Like *Eternal Sunshine of the Spotless Mind* this shit. Start over, erase her from my brain, erase every memory from the past few years and, you know. Do it again. But better."

I exchange a look with Oliver. He nods. *See what I mean?*

Oh, I am seeing it. It's depressing. I know Oliver is just as bent out of shape as Trevor. I mean, they were all friends, albeit Rowan just showed up out of thin air and became a part of their found family. And then, in an instant, she disappeared. Fucked both of them up.

But Oliver doesn't have the romantic heartbreak to deal with. That's a helluva different feeling.

"Look, man. That's not happening," Oliver says, slapping Trevor on the back and then looking to me for a little assistance.

"Why are we hiding back here playing darts on a Saturday night? We should be at the bar," I say with a smile.

"I can't even think about girls right now, Keifer," Trevor sighs.

"Keifer's right. You haven't even tried. Best way to get over someone is to get under someone else, right?" Oliver frowns. "Right?" He wouldn't have too much experience with that. He's the once in a blue moon type of person. I don't know how he deals with it. I have urges all the time that need to get sated. I don't want to think about my brother's sex life, but it is a mystery to me.

I grab Trevor by the arm. "Come on! Let's rip of the band-aid!"

Trevor groans the whole way back into the bar. We've been holed up playing darts since we got here. Now, it's the middle of a rush. Every seat at the bar is taken, but we manage to find high-top to stand around and scan the vicinity.

"See anything?" I ask Oliver. After all, he's the tallest of us and has the best chance of spotting someone for our purposes.

"Guys, seriously, I'm not ready."

"It's just sex, relax," I say, patting him on the back.

"Nothing's just sex," Trevor grumbles.

Oh, buddy, I know that life. Sex always comes with some sort of baggage. For me, it was an unplanned pregnancy and lots of complicated feelings. For Trevor, though, it'll probably just be a girl waking in his bed and a bellyful of regret.

"How about over there?" Oliver nods toward the end of the bar. There's a group of four girls all toasting with tequila shots before knocking them back. "They look like they're trying to have fun tonight."

"I'm not looking to have fun. I want to go home."

I slap Trevor on the back. "Jesus, you're a sad sack!" I'm honestly kind of glad that Trevor is committed to being depressed. It's giving me something else to think about rather than – *Keifer, stop right there. We're not going there tonight. We're having fun, no responsibilities, nothing to think about. Just. Fun.* "I'm going over there. Follow in a minute if it's going well."

I have a way with women. This is a fact. I don't use it for evil. But, if it's not already clear based on previous experience, I have a few charming moves up my sleeve. I approach the girls, and one of them, a redhead, spots me from across the bar. My height doesn't really allow for subtlety, but that's okay, because she taps her friends and whispers to them with a smile.

"Hey! You guys look like you're having fun!" I say jovially.

"What gave that away?" one of them asks. She's got short black hair and green eyes, like a cat.

"Well, I couldn't help but see you doing tequila shots. You want another round? On me?"

They all look at each other nervously until the redhead who spotted me answers with confidence, "Yeah. We'll take another round."

I clap my hands together. "Great! Would you mind if my friends joined us?"

"As long as they're cute," a tiny blonde pipes up.

"And like girls," the dark-haired one adds.

"Trust me. They like girls. And they'll love you. I can

tell." I wave over to Oliver and Trevor. Oliver grabs Trevor practically by the scruff of his neck and drags him our way. "Okay, so...one, two, three, four...seven shots?"

"Damn, you can count."

The girls laugh and so do I. "On a good day. But I've had a bit to drink already, so give me a break, huh?"

The dark-haired woman raises an eyebrow. "I don't give anyone breaks."

Holy shit. Okay, she's intense and I like it. But...a beautiful woman just makes me think about the most beautiful woman I know.

Dara.

"Aha. Okay." I shrug her off, trying not to be mean, but also don't want to give her the impression I'm interested. "This is my older brother, Oliver–"

"Whoa, you're tall," the redhead says and immediately gravitates toward Oliver.

Oliver's body goes rigid as she touches his arm. "Uh. Yeah. Six seven to be precise."

She gapes. "Jeez. How does it feel to see the world from all the way up there?"

"And this is Trevor." I yank him forward. He tries to hide behind my shoulder. "He's not as tall and he's a little shy. Because he's heartbroken.

The tiny blonde and the not-so-tiny blonde coo. "Aww. I'm sorry."

Trevor glances at me. "It's okay. It was a few months ago. I'm getting over it."

I grin. *There he is.* All it takes is a pretty face to get a guy's mojo back. "Okay. Seven shots, coming up."

"Don't take them all yourself," the dark-haired girl says.

I try not to shiver. The old Keifer would have been all

over that. But now, it's just scaring me. Not because she's doing anything wrong. I'm just not...feeling it.

What's going on?

I elbow my way up to the bar and flag down the bartender. "Seven tequila shots with lime for me and my friends."

The bartender looks rather annoyed, but I pull out my wallet and add, "Top shelf," slamming down a couple hundred.

That changes his tune in an instant. He races off to get the shots.

"Well, do you pull out the stops for all the girls?"

I look over my shoulder. The dark-haired girl followed me. *Shit.* I'm stuck between her and the bar as I wait for the shots. There's no getting around her. She may not be particularly big or wide, but her presence is impossible to avoid. "Yeah, you know. I like to make friends."

"You just met us. You don't even know our names."

"Uh...what's your name?"

She takes a step toward me. "You first."

"K-Keifer."

"Fiona."

"Like from *Shrek*." It just comes out, but I immediately regret it.

Her eyes widen and then narrow. "Yeah. Like *Shrek*."

"Sorry, I bet you get that all the time."

"It's fine. You can make it up to me, though."

Is she getting closer to me or is that just my imagination? "How would I do that?"

"Well, after we take our shots, you can buy me a drink."

Keifer a few months ago would have leaped at the chance. Hell, Keifer even a few weeks ago would have.

But things have changed. Drastically. And besides the

fact that I'm not feeling her, the thing that's holding me back is this undeniable feeling I have inside me that by doing anything of any sort with this girl, Fiona, would be a betrayal.

I might not be in a relationship with Dara. But damn, I really like her. In fact, I...

"I'm in love with someone."

Fiona jerks her head back and snorts. "That's a weird way to say you're taken."

"Yeah. Sorry, I think I just realized right now."

Instead of being pissed like I thought she'd be, she smiles. "That's really sweet."

"You think?"

"Yeah. What's she like?"

I want to spill my guts about everything. She's funny, kind, totally stunning. She's selfless and driven. She holds me accountable. Most importantly, she's having my children. And while I've winced away from that responsibility, she hasn't. That's too much, though. Instead, I just say, "She's perfect."

"Wow. You've got it bad, huh?" Fiona laughs and punches me in my arm. "Come on. Let's go do a shot."

Fiona and I balance the shots in our hands and bring them back to the group. Everyone is in good spirits. Me especially. I'm riding high, higher than any drink could make me. In this dingy bar with darts in the back, things have never been clearer.

I don't want this anymore. I want Dara. I want a life with her. And our boys. And if she's scared, if I've hurt her by walking away, I'll be patient. I'll wait. I've proven to her already that I can step up. I just have to really fucking do it and not get scared again. I don't think I will. I'm as clear-headed as I've ever been.

The rest of the night is kind of a blur. I'm just around, palling around with my friends, talking with the girls we've met. There's Fiona, the redhead, Emily, and the two blondes, Allie and Drea. And they're great. In fact, Trevor ends up talking a lot with Drea, and it's good to see him smile once in a while. Even if I feel this is as good as it will get tonight, I feel it's a step in the right direction. Oliver is being chatted up by Emily the whole night. He's being very friendly, but I don't think he's picking up on her signals.

From time to time, Fiona checks in on me. "Why're you here?"

"Huh?"

"Why aren't you running home to that girl you love?"

I flush.

"Did you fuck it up?"

I laugh. "Sort of." *Majorly.*

"Mmm. Dumbass."

"I know."

"Well. You can tell her that you were in a room full of pretty girls and not one of them held a candle to her. Even when a really, really, really hot goth chick was hitting on you."

We laugh. I've gotta find a friend for her. She's fun. "I'll think about that."

Trevor goes home alone and I go home with Oliver. He's stumbling, having had a little too much with Emily. I could tell she was trying to drop him a hint, which he did not pick up until I told him and it was too late.

"Man. I always fuck it up."

"Naw. Not always. You're just too nice."

Oliver mopes. A gentle giant through and through.

It's too late for me to go home, and if I did, I'd surely go right to Dara's house and wake her up so I could tell her everything. So, I sleep in Oliver's guest room. I can hear him snoring through the wall.

Even though I'm so tired and can feel the hangover seeping into my brain, I can't close my eyes.

I'm wide awake, thinking about tomorrow.

Because tomorrow, I'm going to do the most important thing I've ever done.

I'm going to show my whole hand and let a woman in. And if she doesn't love me back...

I'm ready to fight for her.

TWENTY-NINE
DARA

My office, which had previously been a mess of papers and receipts and god knows what else, is now clean as a whistle. We've been in here all day going over my expenses, debts, and plans for the bakery. Each thing cleared up quickly with the help of Rye's bank account. With every protest, all Rye had to say was, "Twins, Dara. Hawthorn twins," and that shut me up really quick.

What started as one of the worst days of my life has ended up being one of the most relieving.

My debts are gone. The financial plans for the bakery are clear and taken care of. And I can focus on making the bakery as beautiful as I want it to be with Rye's bank roll.

It feels nice to be taken care of. And not feel guilty for it.

I lean back in the office chair and rest my hands on my belly. The babies are getting more and more active. I'm starting to be able to feel it when I touch my stomach too, not just the fluttering deep inside. I can't help but dread how they're going to be fighting for room in there the bigger they get.

And yet, at the same time, I can't help but smile. They're walking into a beautiful life. Regardless of whether Keifer is a part of it or not, they have a family. Rye will be here for me. She's made that clear.

"Yeah, I'll be home in the morning..." Rye says into her phone as she paces the hallway outside the office. "Everything's fine. I just need to be here..." She glances in at me and smiles.

I want to tell her to go home to her husband and her baby, but I'm feeling selfish. I need her here with me.

"Give Ivy a kiss for me, alright?" She leans on the doorframe. "Love you too. Bye." When she hangs up, she sighs, looking at her phone.

I curl my lips to the side. "If you miss them, you can go home."

"No, it's okay. I haven't spent a night away from Ivy since she was born. She can handle it, I think, but..." Rye swallows. "It's weird."

"I bet."

She smiles tiredly. "You'll know that feeling soon."

I roll my eyes and laugh. "I don't know, I bet I'll be clamoring for a break from two little boys."

"Maybe, but the second you get away, you'll miss them terribly."

I rub my stomach thinking about the future. I think I know what she means. I'm already scared of what it will feel like not to have them inside, right where I can keep them safe all the time.

Not much later, we head to bed, exhausted from the emotions and work of the day. I wake up to Rye curled around my back. It reminds me of our days back in Madison, when the death of my parents was still so fresh and my heart was raw, and we'd sleep in the same bed, filled with memories of our mothers and their love.

Now look at us.

"You sleep okay?" Rye grunts, lifting her head.

"Eh. Fine. My back is giving me some trouble. How about you?"

"Terrible. This mattress is like rocks. I'm getting you a new one. You're going to need the lumbar support."

I laugh and don't even bother protesting. I know it won't work.

Rye wraps her arms around me, spooning me from behind. "Can I?"

"Yeah. Of course."

She puts her hands on my belly. "Hi boys...it's Auntie Rye."

I giggle and nuzzle her closely. She's like the sister I've never had.

"Don't give your mama too hard of a time because your daddy has already done that."

"*Rye.*"

"I'm just being honest!"

The babies start shifting. "Can you feel? They're moving."

"Hmmm..." She feels around. "No. Not yet."

"Ugh."

Rye laughs. "Don't worry. Soon, you'll be wishing they'd settle down. God...twins. I can't even imagine what that's gonna be like."

"Don't remind me."

"Do twins run in your family?"

I sigh. "My grandmother was a twin."

"Ah! It skips a generation!"

"I thought that was an old wives' tale."

"Maybe. Guess it doesn't matter since you're blessed with twins."

I frown. "You think it's a blessing?"

"Well, sure. Don't you?"

I hadn't thought about it like that. "I'm terrified, Rye. Two babies is like double *everything*. I don't know if I can handle it."

"Oh please, of course you can."

"I was just getting used to the idea of having one baby to deal with. But two is like...what if I'm bad at it?"

Rye looks at me like I'm crazy.

"Seriously! What if I'm bad at it?! Then I'm fucking up two kids instead of just one."

"First of all, you're not fucking up any kids. Parenting is hard, but I know you, Dara, you go into everything with love in your heart. That's why your bakery is going to be amazing. Because it comes from that soft and beautiful place inside you."

I smile. "You're going to make me cry."

"*And*...second of all, you have to stop doubting yourself. I know that's easier said than done, but look how far you've come. You moved to Chicago to start a business, you've been working your ass off while *pregnant*, not to mention you chose to *stay* pregnant. And you've let yourself feel something so deep for someone despite the fear they might not feel it back." Rye pushes my hair out of my face. "You're so fucking strong and you have to start acknowledging it."

Damn. She's right. When she lays it all out like that, I sound like an amazing woman.

Maybe I am one.

"Dara!"

Rye and I sit up fast when we hear my name called from outside.

"What the..." I get to my feet and cross to the window that faces the street. My eyes land first on the big black pickup truck in front of the house. *Keifer.*

The cry of my name comes again. "Dara! Are you home?"

I peer down at the front stoop. Keifer is standing at the front door. He takes a step back and then looks up at my window. I pull the curtain closed, turning to Rye with wild eyes. "It's him!"

Rye's already hustling out of the room. "I'll go out the back."

"Wait!" I call after her as I follow her down the hall. "What do I do?"

"What do you mean, 'what do I do?'! You talk to him, of course!" She grabs me by the shoulder and smiles. "You're going to be great. Whatever happens, you have me in your corner." Then she narrows her eyes. "But you have to call me after and tell me everything."

I nod. "Okay. I will."

Rye kisses my forehead. I follow her down the stairs to the back door. As soon as it shuts behind her, I turn around. I have a clear view of the front door. It seems to creep closer with every passing moment.

Okay, Dara. It's time to face your fears.

From the moment I woke up at the crack of dawn, my mind has been on one thing.

Dara.

I drove back to the cul-de-sac going through all the things I needed to tell her, unable to come up with an appropriate order. I can't believe how badly I've screwed up. Leaving her hanging like that...she doesn't deserve that. Especially now.

I resolved to just let it come out naturally. The way it was supposed to.

But then it crossed my mind she might not even want to see me. That would be her prerogative of course. That didn't mean it wouldn't break my heart.

When I pulled onto the cul-de-sac, I was surprised to see Rye's car, the red SUV Dad bought her before Ivy was born.

Shit. She must know.

I wondered how long she might have known I was the father. Longer than me? Maybe. Girls talk about everything.

I shook off the thought. I could deal with Rye if she was

there to be the protective best friend. We are family, obviously. We care for one another.

I just hope she lets me see Dara.

Now, outside of Dara's front door, I'm desperate to get an answer from her. I know she's home. It's only seven-thirty in the morning, but she's an early riser, even on the weekends. I've woken up to delicious, gourmet scents wafting from her windows in the past.

I've knocked and knocked. And nothing.

So I have to take drastic measures. "Dara!"

I might look like a crazy guy outside her house.

"Dara!"

But I don't care.

"Dara! It's me! I know you're home!"

I need to see her.

I step back and look up into the window of her bedroom at the front of the house. For a split second, I swear I see her in the window. The curtain shifts. She's seen me.

I keep knocking and calling her name until finally the door unlocks. I've worked up a sweat just trying to get her to come to the door. I'm panting from screaming out her name. *Shit, I should have showered or changed or –*

The door flies open. I expect her to look angry or like she's been crying, but it's neither.

She's radiant. Clearly just having roused from sleep, her hair has been merely brushed through with her fingers. She wears a simple white night dress that's thin enough that the sun makes it nearly see through. Her beautiful breasts, her round tummy.

Because of me.

I've lost all ability to speak. My heart is thumping as hard as it ever has. She's taken my breath away. And I'm scared.

"Hi, Keifer."

In her voice, I can hear it. Resignation. She's ready for me to let her go. What else could she have done in this day apart but prepare for heartbreak. That only makes me love her more. I want to give her everything I have in me, so she never has to worry about losing me again. That's not easy to say, though.

"You want to talk?"

"Y-yeah, yes, sorry, I'm nervous," I blurt.

Dara smiles and nods. "Me too. Why don't we go sit and–"

"I'm bad at committing to things."

Her eyebrows jump.

"Relationships and settling down have always scared me. You know, I'm scared of feeling stuck."

Dara nods and slides her hand down her stomach. "Sure."

Fuck, this isn't coming out right: "What I mean is...I don't ever actually feel stuck, I just get scared I'm going to."

Dara's about to respond, but is interrupted by the sound of a car starting. I turn around to see Rye's red SUV peeling out of the cul-de-sac and down the street. Damn, that was pretty stealth.

"I think that's normal, Keifer. I don't blame you."

I wish she wasn't expecting me to let her down. Now it makes it harder to come up with the right thing to say.

I guess the only right thing to say, though, is what's in my heart. Things I don't tend to speak about. Because I'm afraid. Or ashamed. Whatever. "I had this fling in college."

"Keifer, really, you don't have to defend your decision. It's fine. I have help."

"No, no, just listen. I need to get it out. And it might not make any sense, but I promise there's a point. I know you have no reason to trust me but trust me on this."

Dara crosses her arms and leans on the doorframe. She's listening.

Make it count, Keif. "So, college. My last year. You know, I was a very stereotypical college guy. I'm not always proud of how I acted, but I was young and...immature. Anyway, senior year. I had this fling with this girl. Only a couple of months. But it fizzled out. You know, I just lost interest and kinda moved on without explanation."

I'm not doing myself many favors explaining this story. I wonder if when I'm done, she'll tell me I deserved it. I clear my throat. "Anyway, I started seeing her everywhere. Places I hadn't seen her before. We had completely different majors and were rarely in the same buildings on campus before. And suddenly, she was everywhere. She even transferred into one of my classes. It was weird but seemed like a coincidence."

Dara tilts her head to the side, her hair looking like pure gold in the sunlight. It almost completely distracts me from the story I'm telling.

"Um. So. It really stopped seeming like a coincidence when she started showing up to the fraternity, claiming she had thought there was an event going on and there wasn't. And at parties, girls I'd say hi to and that would smile at me and talk to me for a bit would inexplicably later run if I even looked at them. But she'd always be there, lingering around. Eventually, girls started to avoid me altogether at parties and at campus. Sometimes, if she was around, if I even looked in the direction of another girl, she'd make a scene. Like throwing things or screaming at me or at the girl. Or even fainting and... God, it was just crazy."

I chew on the inside of my cheek. "At first, I was really

annoyed. We were done, so what right did she have to be doing that, you know? But as time went on, things got worse and I started to get really scared. I stayed in my room most of the second semester. I attended all the mandatory classes, because I had to, but I avoided going outside my room otherwise because I didn't want to run into her. I had a bunch of locks put on all the doors, even my bedroom door and..." I sigh.

"One night, a friend of mine came knocking on my door. And when I opened the door, there she was with him. I tried to keep her out, but I didn't want to hurt her." I'm shaking as I remember that afternoon. "She forced her way in telling him thanks, and he just left. I was frozen. I knew she was up to something and I just wanted her gone, so I asked her to leave. She said she was moving into my room with me. That we were meant to be together and that she was never letting me go again. She started undressing and told me she loved me and wanted to show me how much. She ordered me to close the door, but I couldn't. I couldn't move. And when I didn't, she reached into her bag and pulled out a knife." I closed my eyes. I had been terrified then. So scared that I was going to die because I was in shock and unable to move.

"What happened?" she whispered, touching my arm and pulling her hand back again.

"I had scheduled a study session for that afternoon, and my friend got there when she was walking toward me with the knife at the ready. He pulled me out and shut the door with her inside. He saved my life that day." My eyes meet hers for a second. "I never pressed charges and I don't know what happened to her after she was taken by security from my room. Maybe she transferred or something. Maybe went on to study abroad. I don't know. But...

I never shook the feeling that she'd just show up out of nowhere."

I glance over at my house. "Still to this day, if I hear a weird noise, I think it might be her. Which is *insane*, I know, but–"

"No, Keifer, it's not insane. That must have been really scary. Must *still* be scary."

I clear my throat. "Anyway, when you showed up right next door, I couldn't help but remember that time. It freaked me out. I know now that that wasn't your intention, obviously. It was all just miscommunication, but that's why I pushed you away so hard. I'm sorry for all that."

Dara giggles, a slight sadness in her tone. "You've already apologized for that, Keifer. There's nothing to forgive, it's okay."

"I'm not just sorry for that, I'm sorry for all of it. Ever since the day I came home, everything you do I get the irrational feeling you're doing in order to keep me. Getting pregnant, having twins–"

"Okay, *that's* insane."

"Right, exactly! It's completely illogical. And I've been putting all that burden on you. Like *you* did something. When in fact it has everything to do with me and how scared I am to let anyone in. How scared I am for things to change and to not be in control of what's going on in my life."

Dara lowers her eyes. "I can see how two babies out of nowhere can throw you for a loop, then."

"Maybe. But the way I've run away from you? It's just not acceptable for a man to do that."

"We all get scared."

I shake my head. "That doesn't mean it's okay to run."

She's quiet.

"I want to be there for you. For our sons." Saying that out loud strikes fear to my core, but I know it's temporary. I know my joy outweighs that. "I'm not gonna run anymore."

Dara smiles. "I'm happy to hear that."

"I'll be here for whatever you need. Whenever you need. I promise."

She rests her hands on the top of her stomach tenderly. "I don't want to hold you back, Keifer."

"That's not–"

"No, listen, if you're committed, then that's what matters to me. You don't need to feel tied down. If you need to jet off and go on an adventure or whatever, I'm not going to stop you. As long as you come back for them, then that's all I care about. They'll always be here when you're done."

I take a deep breath. She's already thinking like a mother. Putting our boys first. Their feelings. Their need for love. It just makes me love her more.

"What about you?"

"What about me?" Dara asks with a frown.

"Will you always be here too?"

She laughs. It tinkles light on the summer breeze. "Well, of course. I'm their mother. Someone has to be here."

"No, that's not what I mean." I reach out and take her hands. Dara tries to draw away, but I caress her hands softly and she settles into my touch. "Will you be here when I come back?"

This time, she seems to understand. "If...if you want me to be."

My smile trembles with emotion. "I do. I really do. This day away from you was like hell, Dara. Because I'm totally falling in love with you."

THIRTY-ONE

DARA

I can't believe my ears. *Keifer might be falling in love with me?* It takes everything in me not to start jumping up and down at the sound of that.

"That might be a lot to hear, but –"

"No, Keifer. I… I feel the same way."

His green eyes widen. "Really?"

I nod, an unbridled smile spreading across my lips. "I thought I was crazy for feeling that. But knowing that you're –"

"A hundred percent. I'm totally falling for you, Dara."

Our joy is reflecting in each other's faces like a mirror, so much so that we both suddenly get bashful and look away.

"What do we do now?" I ask softly.

"I don't know. I'm kinda just in shock you still like me after I ran off the other day."

"Yeah, me too."

Keifer laughs. "Okay. I deserved that."

"Yeah, I'm gonna give you shit for a while about that."

"Good. I look forward to it."

Our eyes meet again.

"We'll start slow," Keifer says softly.

"Baby steps."

He grins. "Yeah. Baby steps." Keifer touches my cheek tenderly. "I'm here, Dara. I'm really here. Nothing can scare me off. Even if we find out it's triplets."

I guffaw loudly. "Please don't put that energy into the universe, I'm still processing carrying two babies for four more months."

Keifer twirls a lock of my hair around his finger. "God, you're so beautiful."

"No..."

"What do you mean *no*?" he asks. "You're beautiful, Dara. The most beautiful woman in the world."

"That's a lot to take in."

"You don't have to believe me for it to be true."

I guess all that matters is that Keifer believes it. I only care about being beautiful in his eyes. Because we might belong to each other one day. Fully, beautifully. A family. I'm still in shock at the possibility. After being alone for so long, I could never have back what I've lost. But maybe I can have something new. Someone who loves me. Two babies. The dearest things I've ever created. Even if it was an accident.

The babies start to shift inside me. The feeling is more intense than it's been thus far. I gasp and look down.

"What is it? What's wrong?" Keifer asks, immediately assuming the worst.

"Nothing, nothing, I... here." I take one of his hands and put it against my stomach. We are both quiet as I slide it across my belly like it's an ultrasound until I find a small flutter. "Do you feel that?"

Keifer waits.

"Close your eyes and focus."

He does. A breeze fondles the tendrils of his hair.

"Talk to them."

"Huh?"

"Say something. They like it when I talk to them."

"Okay. Um. Hey guys."

I laugh. "Starting off strong there."

"Don't judge me, I'm trying!"

I rub his hand encouragingly.

"I'm your dad. And I know I haven't been the best at showing it, but I love you. I love you both. So much."

Come on, babies. Do it for Daddy.

We feel it at the same time, a soft kick right into the palm of Keifer's hand. His eyes shoot open. "Oh my god! Was that it?"

I nod.

There are a few more flutters that he follows around on my growing belly. Each one bringing a bigger smile to his face. "Wow, that's amazing."

"Isn't it?"

"Yeah it's... You're amazing."

I don't refute him He's right. I am amazing.

"I don't deserve you, Dara. I really don't."

I cup one of his hands to my belly and touch his cheek. "Yeah, you do."

And finally, after all this time resisting, of not knowing, we kiss. It pounds with adoration and eagerness. *Now*, we're beginning. Finally. So many false starts or things that should have been endings.

I can't believe we made it here.

Keifer pulls away and looks into my eyes. I see the fire of want burning in his widening pupils.

And god, I want him too.

Slowly, he pushes me up against the door frame, resting his arm over my head. "Is it weird I've never wanted you more than right now?"

I tilt my head back. "Not at all."

Keifer kisses me again. Everything throbs inside me. Eager for his body and his worship. It's just as intense as that first time we met when we needed to fuck so bad we almost did it right there where anyone could see us.

Except this time, we know each other's names. And we adore each other. And there's a future here.

So much future. Years of it.

Keifer propels me inside without much force, shutting the door behind us. He pulls at the hem of my nightgown, fingers trailing up my thighs to my hips to my waist where his hands spread across my swelling sides. "Dear god, Dara. Your body is incredible."

I nearly laugh. Us girls spend so much time worrying about being skinny, but here I am, five months pregnant, wanted beyond comprehension.

Just shows you that attraction is based on much more than what's on the cover of a magazine.

"Take it off," I whisper breathlessly.

He pulls the nightgown over my head and tosses it to the side. His eyes fall to my breasts. They've grown a lot recently and he can tell. "Goddamn, girl."

I giggle.

"Where'd you get these?" he asks playfully, cupping them softly.

"I think you might have had something to do with it."

"Me? Jeez. Well, thank you, me."

I laugh and watch as he pushes a thumb against my nipple. My body seizes.

"Is that okay? Are you tender?"

"Yeah, but... it feels really good."

Keifer breathes in. "Seriously?"

"Yeah, keep... doing that..." Just his touch on my nipples is turning me on so bad.

Keifer starts to kiss my neck, continuing to caress my breasts. His touch is enthralling me. My clit sings the more he stimulates my nipples and I let him know just how much I like it, moaning and groaning as pleasure undulates through my body.

He presses a line of kisses from my neck all the way down to my breasts, eventually engulfing one of my nipples in his mouth. He lifts his eyes to mine. *Is this okay?*

I nod. "Yeah, yeah... holy shit."

As he works my nipple in his mouth, his hand slides between my thighs. His fingers start to dance inside me, deeper and deeper, until he's able to hit my g-spot.

"Fuck, that feels so good." I ram my pussy down onto his hand. "Keep going."

My knees are growing weak as he finger fucks me and sucks on my nipples, but for some reason, I trust him entirely. I won't fall. No matter what, he won't let me fall.

"Oh god, Keifer, I'm going to..."

His mouth revs on my body like a car motor and I burst onto his hand.

I scream in pleasure, clinging to him so I don't just crumple to the ground. "Fuck, fuck, fuck..."

Keifer tears his lips away from my breasts and kisses me. "Goddamn, you're so sensitive."

I go limp in his arms and he laughs, holding me tight. "Fuck, that felt so good."

Keifer cradles me there as if I'm a child. He tenderly kisses the shell of my ear and breathes in my scent. "God, you make me totally feral, Dara."

I sigh happily.

"You did before, but now that you're pregnant, I'm just..." His hand slides down to my belly. "What the hell am I going to do with you?"

I let my head loll back. "You're gonna take me upstairs and fuck me."

"You bet I am."

Once we're upstairs in my room, Keifer makes sure I'm totally comfortable. Extra pillows and everything. He's already doing such a good job of taking care of me.

I watch him cross the room to close the curtains, unbuttoning his shirt as he does so. There's something so simple about watching him undress. Easy. We don't need to do the hungry tug of war for nakedness anymore. We've done that.

Now, it's about so much more.

He pulls his pants down and comes to the end of the bed entirely nude. I'm focused on his hard cock, the head red and dripping. But he's totally focused on me. Measuredly, he mounts the bed and crawls toward me. As if he's never touched me, he touches the inside of my thigh. I pull my legs wider for him.

"I won't hurt you?"

"No, totally the opposite."

He chuckles shyly.

"You just have to be careful."

"I can be careful."

And he is. He shifts my hips back and kneels before me, throbbing at my entrance. I hum in excitement. "Come on, Keifer. I need you."

"I'm just taking it in. Taking *you* in."

I nudge my hips closer to his. My heavy belly makes it harder, but I still have a bit of agility left.

Keifer dips the head into me and lets out a long breath. "Oh, fuck, you feel good."

We get into a good rhythm fast due to my wetness and how relaxed we both are. Keifer's hands rest on my hips until it gets to be too much. He touches my belly and his arousal doubles. "I did this to you."

"You did."

His eyes flick up to mine and he smiles through his lust.

"My body is yours."

"Fuck yes, it is."

"And everyone knows. I can't hide it anymore. I need everyone to know."

He drives harder, turned on beyond belief.

"When they see us together, they'll know that you claimed me."

"Jesus, Dara." I can tell he's holding back, afraid to go too fast given my condition.

"Just go. Just do it."

"I'm scared."

"It's okay, I'll be okay. The babies will be –"

"No, I feel like I'm going to cry, I don't want..." He trails off and pauses in his thrusting momentarily.

I've cried after sex before. The feelings have been so intense that it just comes bubbling out. But I've never seen a man cry after sex. "You can cry. It's okay."

"It just feels so good. And you're so amazing and I –" He hangs his head, hiding his face.

"Keifer, look at me."

He does, shame in his wet eyes.

"I'm so happy that you're the father of my babies. There's no one I'd rather do this with. I promise."

Keifer blinks and tears run down his face.

I interlace my fingers with his on my belly. "Let yourself feel as good as I do. Because I feel fucking amazing."

Keifer nods and tentatively returns to pushing himself inside me.

"Yes. God, yes. You're going to make me come again."

"Oh my fucking god, oh my–" Keifer loses control, pounding into me as if some otherworldly force is in charge of his body until he thrusts once more and releases.

I join him, both of us letting out primal grunts of pleasure. My body feels like it's on fire. Not just from my orgasm, but from his touch. It's like he's burning me.

"Are you alright?" he asks, face stained with tears.

"Amazing, Keifer."

"You promise? You're okay?" He leans forward and cups my belly in his hands. "Is everything..."

"Yes, I promise."

We unlock from each other and cuddle up together in the pillows, arms wrapped around each other. He won't stop touching my stomach, as if by touching it, he can protect our babies.

"See, doesn't it feel nice to let go?" I ask softly, kissing his chin that's budding with stubble.

"God, yes. It feels so good to let go."

Our eyes meet, and for some reason, I think he's talking about much more than letting go of an orgasm.

"I'm here, Dara."

"I know."

"I'm not going anywhere. I'm not going to run anymore."

I touch his chest. His heart is beating steady and clear. "It's alright if you do."

"No. Listen to me. I'm not running anymore. I'm here

for you. For our boys. This is... this is my life now. And I've never wanted anything more."

"Not even an anonymous one-night stand after a wedding?"

Keifer blushes. "Sounds like you're talking from experience."

"It's just a hypothetical."

Keifer shakes his head. "Dara, sex with a stranger doesn't make me feel nearly half as good as I feel right now."

I beam up at him. "I'm so falling in love with you."

"I'm not so sure I'm falling anymore. I might have already hit the ground."

I kiss him deeply. Meaningfully. He's not going anywhere. And neither am I.

When we part, Keifer looks at me shyly. "I know we're taking baby steps..."

"Yes?"

"And I'm committed to that."

"Says the man who just implied he loved me."

"Implied being the keyword."

I roll my eyes and start to wriggle out of his arms, but he holds me there. "Kidding, kidding."

"You better be."

Keifer's gaze hardens in mine. "Says the guy who loves you."

There. It's out in the open.

"But today is Sunday. And my family always has dinner together on Sunday. I know you've been there too. But we've never been together. And I want them to know as soon as you're comfortable that we're..." He strokes my stomach and looks down. "Fucking twins, Dara!"

I laugh.

Keifer sighs. "It's all going to go so fast. I just want them to be a part of it."

I hesitate. The past five months have been a crazy whiplash. Lovers, strangers, enemies, lovers, friends, enemies, lovers again...more. Am I ready to invite other people in?

"When you're ready. We don't have to do it tonight."

Rye already knows. Why hold back? "No. I want to go."

"Really?"

"Yes. Let's do it."

Keifer kisses me, the excitement plain as day on his face. Then, he goes to my belly and whispers, "Did you hear that, guys? It's a big day for us!"

I laugh and stroke his hair as he coos to the babies.

"You're going to get to meet everyone. Your uncles and grandpa, Auntie June, all your cousins..."

I don't let the anxiety of meeting Keifer's entire family bother me. It's clear there's so much love in his family. I don't think there's a reason for me to be scared.

This is it. This right here is my family.

And it's about to get bigger.

I don't tell my family ahead of time. I know it'd be better to give them proper warning, but I want to be able to look at them when I tell them about Dara. I want to be able to answer any questions in person and have them see the happiness resonating from me.

That doesn't mean that I'm not fucking nervous, though.

We both are. The drive up to my dad's home in Wilmette is quiet, though we have the radio playing softly the whole way. I have Dara's hand in mine the whole way there, softly caressing it with my thumb. She looks absolutely gorgeous. A white, floral dress that drapes down her body like she's an angel. Light makeup. A perfume that smells like vanilla and honeysuckle.

She's divine. From heaven. My Eve.

It took her forever to pick out an outfit; everything she felt comfortable in was an attempt at concealing her belly even though she is well past having that ability in her pregnancy.

I can tell she's self-conscious, though. Her protruding

belly means that it's going to be obvious to everyone immediately upon seeing her.

Luckily, Dara already has a history with Dad and Rye and has met everyone else at the wedding and that one time she joined the family for dinner when I was out of town.

So much has changed now.

Once we pull up to the house, it's clear everyone is already there. That's how I wanted it. Easier to get it all out in the open.

I pull into the round drive and turn off the ignition. "Will you be okay waiting here for a couple of minutes?" I ask.

Dara looks at me and nods, but her eyes betray her attempt at composure.

"You don't have to be scared. They're going to be happy." I'm saying this more for myself than for her. I kiss her hand. "I know I haven't earned it yet, but please trust me."

She smiles. "I do."

Before I get out of the car, I kiss her. Her lips are soft and inviting. I could kiss them forever.

And I will.

I leave her in the car, straightening out my dress shirt as I go inside. Family dinners are usually a pretty casual affair, but this is a big day. It only makes sense I take it seriously in every way possible.

I let myself inside and follow the sound of voices all the way through the house to the terrace. Dad and Jarred are grilling, the kids are playing out on the lawn with June, Trevor and Oliver are talking together softly, and Rye is arranging a summer bouquet on the table. She's the first one to see me.

I know she knows just by looking at me from the way she smiles. "Hey, Keif."

"Hey, Rye. Did I see your car at the cul-de-sac earlier today or was that my imagination?"

She shrugs. "You must be seeing things."

I chuckle. "Yeah. Maybe."

From the look she's giving me, I can tell she wants more information. *In due time, Rye.* "Um, hey everyone!"

Dad and Jarred turn from the grill. Dad waves the tongs at me. "There he is!"

"Late as usual," Jarred adds with a roll of his eyes.

"Uncle Keifer!" Piper squeals and runs over to me excitedly, wrapping her arms around me.

I've been avoiding the kids to keep a clear head, but the moment I feel Piper's hug, my heart grows ten sizes.

I can't wait for this to be my life. My two boys and Dara.

All nestled into my family.

I bend down and give her a kiss. "Hey, honey. Could you tell your mommy to come over for a second?"

She nods and runs to the lawn. I watch June listen to her and then look over at me quizzically.

"Um, I have an announcement to make."

Recognition crosses her face. She gets up from the lawn and comes closer to the terrace, her eyes trailing back from time to time to keep an eye on the kids.

"What's up, Keif?" Oliver asks, kicking back in his seat.

I scan my family. The one that's grown exponentially in just two years. "It's hard to believe that just a couple years ago, this family looked really different."

Dad and Jarred exchange a look. Bewildered and concerned. They are the main reason why things have shifted as much as they have.

"But it's changed so much. In a really good way." I look

to June and then to Rye. "I promise." I take a deep breath. "I guess I'll just come out with it and say it. Uh..." I run my hand through my hair. "I've found someone too."

Everyone alights with gasps and excitement. Even Rye and June play along despite knowing bits and pieces of the story.

"That's fantastic, Keifer. Who's the girl? When can we meet her?" Dad is alight with questions.

I clear my throat. "Actually, you've already met her. She's Rye's friend. Dara."

Dad looks to Rye in surprise and she avoids his gaze.

"We met at June and Jarred's wedding and..." *Keep going, you're almost there.* "To make a long story short, she's pregnant."

More shocked gasps. Jaws drop, eyes grow wide.

"Five months along, actually."

I expected my family to be happy, but the way my brothers and Dad crowd around me with excitement and congratulations is more than my heart can handle. There is no question of their happiness for me, no worry that I can't handle it or shouldn't be a father.

It's just the Hawthorn way.

"You guys really need to learn about birth control. Jesus Christ," Oliver needles.

"I think it's a little late for that," Jarred says, slapping me on the back.

"Really late, actually." Everyone looks at me in confusion. "We're having twins."

June screams and grabs onto Rye. Rye's dropped all pretense, nodding enthusiastically. "Do you know the gender?" June asks.

June. My best friend. I've lost her a bit along the way. She's been so involved in her new family. Her baby boy.

And I've been burying myself deeper and deeper into fear and shame. The moment she looks at me, I really feel like I've come home. "Two boys."

She screams again and barrels over to me, throwing her arms around my neck. "Our babies can be friends. They'll be best friends."

I laugh and hold her tightly. "Cousins, even."

"Oh, shut up." She kisses my cheek, looking back to Jarred, her husband, with teary eyes.

When the smoke has cleared from her excitement, Dad swoops in beside me, pulling on my shoulder for me to face him. He's got a look in his dark green eyes, one I so rarely see now that I'm an adult. Like I'm precious and little. "Are you happy?"

I nod vigorously. "Yes. I'm really happy."

He closes the space between us and hugs me tight, slapping me on the back. "Congratulations."

I hug him tightly. I can't help wishing that Mom were here too. That wish never goes away, but sometimes it gets louder.

When Dad pulls away, there are tears in his eyes. "So, where is she?"

"In the truck," I say bashfully.

"Well, go get her, don't leave her in there! What's wrong with you?" June scolds, waving me away.

I don't waste a moment. I sprint through the house to the truck. When I throw open the door, Dara looks at me with wide eyes. "Oh god, did it go badly?"

"What?! What, no!"

"Then why did you open the door like that?"

"Like what?"

"Like something's wrong!"

"Nothing's wrong, they all want to see you!"

Dara's alarm settles. "Oh."

"Yeah, it's a good thing. I just got... excited."

She laughs and touches my cheek. "It's good?"

"Yeah. It's great, Dara."

Her hazel eyes search my face for any hint that I'm lying. I don't blame her. I'll earn her implicit trust one day. "I'm scared."

"But they already love you."

"I know, but I'm just..." Dara smooths out the fabric over her bump. "I'm scared, Keifer." She looks over my shoulder at the front door. "Once we walk through that door, once everyone sees me and everyone knows... then *it's real.*"

I smile, joining my hand with hers on her belly. "Don't you want it to be real?"

"Yes, but... what if it all gets taken away from me? What if it all disappears?"

I wish I could tell her it won't be. But that would imply I had any sort of control over life and its designs. "I think that's the chance we take when we love anyone." I lean closer to her. My words are just for her. "I'm here *now*. And I'm not going anywhere unless something happens to me. That's what I can promise you. And I can promise you they all feel the same. They're going to love you." I glance down at her stomach. "All of you."

Dara laughs and looks down at her stomach with me.

"You ready?" I ask.

She takes a deep breath and nods. "As I'll ever be."

I had no reason to worry. The moment Dara walks out onto the terrace, she is inundated with love and affection from my whole family. It helps that Rye is there. At dinner, I sit on one side of her while Rye sits on the other. From time to time, they giggle to each other at some secretive words they exchange between themselves. Rye leans across Dara to me at one point and says, "You better be good to her. No more making her cry."

When I hear that, I wrap my arm around Dara protectively. "Never again. Promise."

Rye rolls her eyes and smiles.

No one asks too many questions. There'll be plenty of time for that. But Dara *is* the center of attention. She relays everything about her upcoming bakery, going into business with Rye, and her excitement about motherhood. "I have to admit, twins is pretty..." she glances at me, "...daunting. But once I got over the initial shock, I couldn't believe our luck. Twice as much to love, you know?"

When she puts it like that, I can't help but agree.

June watches me from across the table like a proud mom, balancing now eight-month-old Hayden on her lap. "Proud of you," she mouths.

"Thanks," I mouth back. It's only fair that since I'm the godfather of her son, she is godmother to mine. Our children will have built in family playmates. What could be better than that?

Once dinner is finished, we all move out onto the lawn to rest while the kids go back to playing. Ivy is now big enough to run around with Piper, even if she's stumbling, and Piper even manages to include little Hayden in all her games.

Dara and I sit together, chatting with June and Jarred. Our first time as a couple being seen by other people. We are shy with one another, but tender. Small touches, little looks.

"How are you feeling?" I ask her.

"Good."

"Are you tired?"

Dara shakes her head. "I'm having too nice of a time to be tired."

I smile. "Good, that's good."

She leans into me, using my front as a place to rest. The world is glowing in twilight and the children laughing is like music.

"Mommy!" Piper calls out and rushes over to June, Ivy following behind her. Hearing Piper be able to call someone "mommy" is one of the best gifts our whole family has gotten. Made even sweeter by the fact that June was already a part of our tribe.

June welcomes Piper into her arms. "What is it?"

Piper whispers something into June's ear. June looks at me and Dara. "I don't know, honey. You'd have to ask."

"Can you ask?"

June shakes her head. "You're a big, brave girl. You can ask. And if she says no, that doesn't mean you did a bad thing."

Dara and I exchange a glance.

The little girl comes over to Dara. "Dara?"

"Yes, honey?" Dara smiles.

"Could we feel your tummy?"

"Oh!" Dara says in surprise.

"You can say no. It's okay," June says.

Dara shakes her head. "That's okay. Yeah. You can feel. You just have to be gentle."

I pick Ivy up on my lap while Piper wedges herself next to Dara. "Actually, the boys really like when you talk to them. They might move for you. But you have to be patient."

"Hi boys!" Piper yelps.

Ivy laughs and so does everyone.

Piper grins. "I'm your cousin and I'm a big sister. I'm the biggest one around here actually. So, I'll take care of you."

I guide Ivy's hand tentatively to the other side of Dara's stomach.

Dara cups both hands to her belly. "That was really nice, Piper. Maybe try something like this." Dara cranes her neck lower and coos softly, "Hi boys. It's Mommy. Can you believe how loved you already are?"

I have to look away and gain my composure. So much has happened in the past day. It's been a whirlwind. I can barely believe it's real. June rubs my back.

"I know it's been a long day, but maybe you can say hi to Piper and Ivy?"

Dara, Piper, and Ivy are quiet. Waiting. Then, Ivy lets out an excited squeal, pulling her hand away from Dara's stomach. "Baby!" she says. Her ability to speak is coming in fast these days, even if her consonants are mushy.

"I want to feel, I want to feel!" Piper anxiously cries out.

"Shhh..." Dara rubs her hand. "We just need patience." Dara looks to me and then takes my hand. "You know what? The twins love their daddy. Maybe Uncle Keifer can help you."

I rest my hand near Piper's. My niece smiles hopefully at me. Maybe I'm her ticket to feeling a little flutter. "They like it when you whisper something sweet." I did that all day after Dara and I consummated our newfound connection. I couldn't get enough of feeling the boys bouncing around in her womb, however soft it was. I lean close to Dara's belly and whisper. "Hi babies."

"Hiiii babies," Piper repeats.

"I love you so much. We all love you so much."

"I love you the most," Piper whispers.

Dara laughs, stroking Piper's dark blonde curls.

A moment later, I feel a little movement against my fingers and so does Piper. She doesn't squeal or cry out, but her eyes get big. "Wow. Two whole babies."

I nod. "Two whole babies. Crazy, right?"

Dara touches the back of my neck. I look to her, eyes falling to her pink lips. "Two whole babies," she echoes.

"That's a lot of babies," I reply.

"Two too many?"

I shake my head and kiss her softly. "Just the right amount."

EPILOGUE

DARA

Nine months later…

It's amazing how time flies when you're having twins and opening a new business.

And having fun. Can't forget the fun.

March. Opening day of my bakery. Right next door to Rye's flower shop, just as we planned. Most people might think I'm crazy to open a business just five months after giving birth. And they might be right!

But I'm also ecstatic.

It's eight-forty-five in the morning. Doors open for the Grand Opening of Daisy's Delights at nine. The menu has been finalized, the community has been notified, and everything is going off without a hitch.

Well, almost.

"What is that smell?!" I rush into the kitchen to find one of the state of the art ovens pouring out smoke. When I pull it open, there's a whole pie burnt to a crisp inside. I cover my mouth with a rag and start to wave my hand around the clear the air of smoke. "Fuck."

"Everything okay?" Keifer pokes his head in from the

door. He's got one of our sons, Danny, named for my father, strapped to his front.

"Does it look okay?" I retort.

Keifer shields Danny's little face from the oncoming deluge of smoke. "Damn. What happened?"

I pull the pan out of the oven and rush to dump the decrepit, ashy pie into the trash. "Just lost track of time. Something. I don't know. I'm always doing that these days." I've been foggy ever since my ninth month of pregnancy. Now, I can chalk it up to the exhaustion of taking care of not one, but two babies. Being a mother has been one of the most rewarding things in my life, but no one is exaggerating how exhausting it is. "Now, I'm not going to have a fruit pie for the opening. That's going to ruin everything."

Keifer laughs. "Are you kidding? It's going to be amazing. A fruit pie isn't going to do anything."

"Yes, it is! Pie people can be split into two categories. Fruit pie people and chocolate-slash-everything-else pie people. And if the fruit pie people aren't represented, I'm going to have hell to pay!" I sit heavily on a stool in the corner of the kitchen with a sigh. "This is a disaster."

"Where's Trip?"

I look down at the baby sling that's laying limply over my chest, sans baby Trip. It only made sense to name both our babies after our fathers. Since Keifer's father was the second Ashton in his family, that made ours the third. Trip. For a moment, I panic, clutching my heart. Where could I have lost a baby? Did I toss him in the trash with my pie? But then I remember. "Rye's got him. Oh god. You scared me."

Keifer comes over to me. "Dar?"

"What?"

Danny gurgles, capturing my attention. It's a happy

coo. I smile tiredly and grab his little dangling foot. "Hi, baby." He smiles down at me, saliva dripping from his lips. I rub his toes through his onesie. "Aren't you a happy boy?"

The clock is ticking down, but when I'm with my boys, time stops. Watching them grow has been my greatest privilege. Miraculously, I carried them all the way to term, and, after a long labor, I was blessed with two very happy, bubbly boys.

I feel Keifer run his hand through my hair and my eyes flutter shut.

I've been blessed with Keifer too. My Adam. My rock. Ever since the moment he stepped up, he's never stepped down. He was there at every moment of my pregnancy, through every breakdown after birth, and now is hands on with our boys no matter how much work he has going on at the office.

I couldn't have asked for a better man.

"It's going to be perfect. And no one is going to care about the fruit pie."

I blink my eyes open. "You don't know that."

"I do. And if they're mad, I'll fight them."

I laugh and so does Danny. "Was that funny, honey?"

"Danny, tell Mommy it's all going to be perfect. It's all going to be great."

Just then, an ear-splitting cry rattles the bakery. *Trip*. I leap to my feet and rush into the front where Rye and June have been holding down the fort before we open the doors.

"Shhhh! It's okay, it's okay!" Rye says, trying to soothe Trip.

Though Danny and Trip are identical in looks, they have different personalities. Trip is the drama queen. When he gets inconsolable, he needs me or Keifer. Rye, though, has been committed to trying to get Trip to trust her just as much.

It hasn't been working.

"Trip, honey! Come here! I know, you've missed Mama, haven't you?" I swipe Trip out of Rye's arms and tuck him back into the sling on my chest. I pat his back, shushing him, until he's settled. Then, he blinks open his eyes, staring into my face.

The boys both have green eyes like Keifer's, although just a bit deeper. When I look into them, I get totally swept away. Was it not enough to make them adorable but they had to be beautiful too? What is a mother to do?

"How are you feeling?" Rye asks.

"Fine. I'm fine. How much time do we have?"

June checks her phone. "Five minutes."

"*Five?*" I feel my face getting hot and my heart start to race. "I feel like I'm going to be sick." Trip starts to squall when I stop rocking side to side so I return to that. Never a moment for myself with these two. Not that I'd change it for the world.

Keifer has followed me out into main area of the bakery. "Relax. It's going to be great."

June nods. "Keifer's right. There's no reason to freak out."

"There is every reason to freak out! This is everything! This is my whole life!"

Rye grabs me by the shoulders. "Dara, pull yourself together."

I zip my lips shut and take a deep breath.

"What's the worst that could happen?"

I close my eyes and think. "Someone comes in and takes a bite and then throws it at me. And then they knock over the pastry case. And then they hate me. And the babies cry."

"Well, that sounds like a lawsuit waiting to happen," Keifer mutters.

I laugh. He's always got a wise crack on hand. I need that when I get too in my head. All through my labor he kept my mind off the pain by making me laugh.

"Okay, if that happens, you're not alone. We're all here for you. And realistically, that's not going to happen, and Keifer is right about the lawsuit," Rye says, squeezing my arms.

I open my eyes and look around. "You're right. Time check, June."

"Just one more minute."

I look at the door. "Let's do this."

The grand opening is a success. At least the first two hours. The staff does a phenomenal job while I run the register. Trip and Danny are big hits with the customers. Rye, June, and Keifer work as greeters and chat up customers as they filter in and out. Everyone who comes in is in love with the selection, even though there's no fruit pie. We are opening to rave reviews.

It's thrilling, especially because I'm sharing it with the people I love most.

Over the past nine months, June, Rye, and I have become a dynamic trio. They have been my rocks as a new mother. And we just have a blast. It's good to be able to bond over the whacky Hawthorn boys.

Around noon, I've arranged to close the bakery for an hour so we, as a family, can celebrate. That's when the rest of the clan arrives. Ashton with Ivy, newly two years old, Jarred with Piper and Hayden, along with Oliver. Dear, sweet Oliver is such a good sport now that he's the only guy in the family without a baby (or two). His nieces, nephews, and little sister can't get enough of Uncle Ollie.

Ash immediately comes to me and reaches for Trip. "Let me get a load of these guys, huh?"

"You've got good timing." Now that everyone's here, I have to sneak into the kitchen to grab the cake I've made for the occasion.

Trip melts into Ash's arms.

"Let me help," Keifer says.

"It's okay, it's just one cake."

"No, I'm coming." Keifer hands Danny off to June and follows me into the kitchen.

I giggle. "Seriously, Keif, I've got it."

"You've been on your feet since five this morning. I want you to rest."

I get to the fridge, grab the handle, and give him a look. "Babe, you're sweet, but I'm not pregnant anymore. You don't have to worry so much."

"Of course I have to worry about you! It doesn't matter if you're pregnant or not." He comes up behind me and rubs my shoulders. "I love you. I always worry."

"Love" entered our vocabulary pretty quickly after deciding to give the whole relationship thing a go. We were pitiful at baby steps, rushing into most everything. Although, with two babies on the way, it was hard not to feel rushed. In a little under two months, construction was already underway to unite the two houses on the cul-de-sac into one.

"Let me get the cake for you... You, go rest..." Keifer kisses my forehead.

I melt into his arms. Exhaustion be damned. I still can't get enough of this man. "Fine. You win."

"Good."

I spin out of his arms, carried by his kiss, and go take a seat at one of the tables with Ash and Rye. Trip cranes his neck back, reaching for me when he sees me. Ash sighs. "Ugh. Every time, Dara."

"I'm sorry," I giggle and pull Trip into my lap. "I can't help it." I push my nose up against his and kiss him. He giggles. "I can't help it!"

Suddenly, June is at my side with Danny, handing him over. I think nothing of it. I'm a pro at having a baby in each arm. And I love the feeling of having them both close like this. I miss the times they were rolling around in my belly. Sure, they were in quite close quarters by the end, but I don't think I ever would have had enough of that feeling.

"Alright, here it is!" Keifer announces as he enters, holding up a cake.

I frown. "Keifer, that's not the cake."

"I know."

"You said you'd..." This cake is yellow. I made a beautiful strawberry short cake. I look around frantically to everyone. "I promise, this isn't what I made. I don't even know where you got this."

No one seems to bat an eye as Keifer sets the cake down in front of me.

"Keifer, seriously, what is this?" I'm not amused.

"It's your cake. Well, not *your* cake. But it's a cake for *you*."

"Dara, just look at it!" Rye whispers across the table.

I roll my eyes and look down at the cake. Shock hits me like a tidal wave as I read the words "Will you marry me?" scrawled in pastel purple cursive.

"What?" I turn to look at Keifer.

He's already kneeling before me, pulling something out of his jacket pocket.

"What?!" I ask again, met with giggles from my family around me.

Keifer reveals the ring box. "Dara Palmer. When I met you, I didn't know your name."

I'm stunned. Unable to speak or laugh or even blink.

"But I knew that you were the only woman in the world. Somehow."

Eve. That's what I've been from the beginning to him.

"And even though our love took a while to take root, the moment it did, I knew I was done for."

I pull my sons closer to me. This moment couldn't be more perfect.

"I will admit, I've had a lot of growing up to do. I think I still am, in some ways. I was so scared of losing my freedom. That a baby...then two..." He smiles boldly at our boys. "... would keep me from what I thought I wanted."

Keifer raises his eyes to mine. Steady. "It took me longer than it should have. I know that now. But I've learned the ultimate freedom is to love and be loved. With you, Dara, I found my home, my beacon. The freedom to just be."

He opens the box. A brilliant ring gleams inside.

"We already have so much together. And I want so much more. Will you marry me?"

I'm smiling so big my cheeks hurt. Tears are rushing down my face. "Yes. Yeah. Of course."

Keifer lunges toward me and kisses me. Our boys between us.

The room alights with cheers and laughter. I look around, first finding Rye's eyes. We'll be family in more than just feeling now. Then, I see the rest of them. Jarred, Ash, June, Oliver, the children. I can't believe my eyes. This room, full of love. My bakery, my family. People that soon I'll share a last name with.

I never thought in my wildest dreams that I'd shake the feeling of loneliness.

And here I am. With a man who loves me and two baby boys and a whole, wonderful, huge family.

"What do you think, boys? Can I marry Mama?" Keifer nuzzles his face toward Danny and Trip. Both of them reach for him, giggling at his kisses.

He finds my hand and slips the ring on. I capture his chin in my hand. "What'd you do with the real cake?"

Keifer cackles. I love that laugh. "It's there. Don't worry." He brushes a lock of hair from my face. "I've got you, Dara. Always."